Outback Surgeons

These Outback heroes aren't looking for love, but in the caring country town of Meeraji Lake...it's catching!

Welcome to Meeraji Lake—
where Oscar Price and Felix McLaren find
sharing the doctors' quarters with ice queen
Daisy Forsythe-York and über-friendly
Harriette Jones is the perfect recipe for love...

Find out what happens in
Daisy and Oscar's story

English Rose in the Outback

and

Harriette and Felix's story

A Family for Chloe

Don't miss the **Outback Surgeons** duet
from Mills & Boon Medical Romance author
Lucy Clark

Available in Large Print format
November 2016!

Dear Reader,

Welcome to the second story in my Outback Surgeons series. Harriette and Felix certainly make an interesting couple, and I loved getting to know them.

I knew I wanted to write about a heroine who has an adult son, and the relationship between Harriette and her son Eddie is based on the great friendship I share with my own adult son. Added to this mix is a very strong, some would say stubborn little girl who is almost four. Miss Chloe Jane McLaren was an absolute hoot to create and write about, because when you're almost four years old you know *everything*…except how to juggle! Poor Felix often feels as if he's floundering in a world he knows nothing about, but with Harriette's help, and support from the rest of the crazy characters in the small Outback Australian town of Meeraji Lake, he finally finds his happily-ever-after.

During the writing of this story my beloved father passed away from cancer, which often made my creative times harder to find. I can't thank my editors enough for their patience as I worked through my grief. There are many aspects of this story that pay homage to my dad and what he taught me and my siblings—the main thing being that family really is so very important. Harriette helps Felix to realise this, and to understand that what is past is past and all we can do is learn from our mistakes and move forward with a positive attitude.

A Family for Chloe will always hold a special place in my heart… I hope it finds one in yours, too.

Warmest regards,

Lucy

A FAMILY FOR CHLOE

BY
LUCY CLARK

First published in Great Britain 2016
By Mills & Boon, an imprint of HarperCollins*Publishers*
1 London Bridge Street, London, SE1 9GF

Large Print edition 2016

© 2016 Anne Clark

ISBN: 978-0-263-26131-8

Our policy is to use papers that are natural, renewable and recyclable products and made from wood grown in sustainable forests. The logging and manufacturing processes conform to the legal environmental regulations of the country of origin.

Printed and bound in Great Britain
by CPI Antony Rowe, Chippenham, Wiltshire

19086076

Lucy Clark loves movies. She loves binge-watching box-sets of TV shows. She loves reading and she loves to bake. Writing is such an integral part of Lucy's inner being that she often dreams in Technicolor®, waking up in the morning and frantically trying to write down as much as she can remember. You can find Lucy on Facebook and Twitter. Stop by and say g'day!

Books by Lucy Clark

Mills & Boon Medical Romance

Wedding on the Baby Ward
The Boss She Can't Resist
Taming the Lone Doc's Heart
Diamond Ring for the Ice Queen
Falling for Dr Fearless
A Socialite's Christmas Wish
Dare She Dream of Forever?
One Life-Changing Moment
Resisting the New Doc In Town
The Secret Between Them
Her Mistletoe Wish
His Diamond Like No Other
Dr Perfect on Her Doorstep
A Child to Bind Them
Still Married to Her Ex!

Visit the Author Profile page
at millsandboon.co.uk for more titles.

To Erica, Tim, Ella and Chloe—
wonderful friends, thank you
for allowing me to peek into your lives.

Hebrews 4:16

Praise for
Lucy Clark

'A good and enjoyable read. It's a good
old-fashioned romance and is everything
you expect from medical romance.
Recommended for medical romance lovers
and Lucy Clark's fans.'

—*Harlequin Junkie* on
Resisting the New Doc In Town

'I really enjoyed this book—well written,
a lovely romance story about giving love a
second chance!'

—*Goodreads* on
Dare She Dream of Forever?

CHAPTER ONE

'HARRIETTE? HARRIETTE JONES?' Felix McLaren stood in the middle of the Meeraji Lake District hospital's emergency department and looked around for Dr Harriette Jones, the doctor he was supposed to contact, the doctor who was supposed to be in charge of the small outback Australian hospital. Apparently, she wasn't here. In fact, there didn't seem to be anyone in the entire ED. How could a hospital—one located in the middle of nowhere—be completely empty? He found the notion impossible, especially as he'd always worked in bustling, hectic hospitals.

Felix looked around, astonished to find all the treatment rooms and emergency bays set up and ready for whatever emergencies might befall the small community. What on earth had he got himself into? He'd thought the decision to work in the Australian outback, in a small sleepy town, the right thing to do given his present circumstances;

that working here would afford him more leisure time, but this—this was absolutely absurd. He'd expected things to be quiet but not *this* quiet.

He hitched up the sleeping almost-four-year-old girl in his arms and walked towards one of the treatment rooms. 'Hello?' he called as loud as he dared so as not to wake the child. The last thing he needed right now was for her to wake up. He looked around to see if there was a bell or something he could ring in order to alert someone to his presence. 'Hello? Harriette? Tori? Anyone?' Still he received no answer. He'd been told by his friend Oscar Price to speak to either Harriette or Tori but neither was to be found.

'They'll be on hand to help you with whatever you need,' Oscar had told him. Well, Oscar had been wrong. Felix shook his head with complete incredulity at the situation. What if there was an emergency? What were the patients supposed to do then? Treat themselves? He could only hope the drug cupboard was locked up tight.

Surely there had to be *someone*, somewhere within this thirty-bed hospital, which boasted a small surgery, one ambulance and, from what he could see, two very well-stocked emergency treatment rooms.

He walked back to the nurses' desk and availed himself of a chair, sinking into it with relief. Chloe resettled herself in his arms without incident. Ordinarily she wouldn't have had a bar of him but as she was so completely exhausted, she probably had no idea she was now sleeping in the arms of the guardian she didn't like.

And he knew for a fact that she didn't like him because she'd told him so, in no uncertain terms. The words, 'I hate you' had left her lips several times during their short acquaintance and although he recognised them as the words of a child, that she couldn't possibly comprehend the magnitude of her situation, they'd still cut him deep.

It was the main thing he'd quickly discovered about becoming an instant parent—when it came to the child's feelings about a person, place or thing, they told the absolute, honest to goodness truth. For Chloe, her new guardian was someone she one hundred percent did not like. As far as she was concerned, he was 'dumb'. She'd called him the word because he'd told her he wouldn't be able to help her find her mummy and daddy.

For the most part, though, Felix thought he wasn't doing such a bad job. He usually managed to cope fairly well when she was asleep, but when she was awake Chloe Jane McLaren was more than a handful. Not that he blamed her. The poor little girl had been through more than enough during the past three months. Shunted around, confused, abandoned and now he'd brought her halfway around the world.

Although she'd been born in Lancashire to an English mother and an Australian father, apart from him, Uncle Felix, she really had no other relations. Of course there was Felix's father, but the two men had been estranged for decades. Not only had Felix had to deal with the deaths of his brother, David, and his sister-in-law, Susan, but now he'd become an instant parent.

He was doing his best, trying to give Chloe some sort of normal life and, as such, he'd realised he needed to downsize his own workload. It had been a difficult decision because his career had been his life for so long. He'd worked incredibly hard and incredibly long hours to achieve the success as a respected and sought-after general surgeon. He'd won fellowships, been appointed to boards, written several published papers and been involved with new and innovative inventions designed to make the surgeon's life that much easier. He was considered, amongst his peers, as a brilliant mind. Now…he sighed and shifted the sleeping child a little in his arms. Now, he was responsible for a little person and he'd never felt more out of his depth.

That was the reason why he'd agreed to take the job here, in outback Australia. He'd hoped it would provide him with time. Time to get to know Chloe, time to come to terms with his grief, time to figure out what on earth he was going to do in the future. Would a year here make a difference to his career path? Could he be a respected surgeon *and* a parent? Should he employ a full-time nanny and housekeeper to give Chloe more stability? Or would that make her feel as though she'd been abandoned by yet another person in her life? He'd been so conflicted that when he'd bumped into his old friend Oscar Price, who had been temporarily in England, Felix had found himself confessing he'd no idea what to do. Oscar, as it turned out, was director of Meeraji Lake District Hospital in outback Australia but was presently on leave with his new fiancée, Daisy.

'Why not go to Meeraji Lake for a while?' Oscar had suggested. 'A locum, Harriette Jones, is there holding down the fort but it's a two-doctor hospital and I hate leaving everyone in the lurch. At the moment, though, family comes first and Daisy's mother has been ill—we're planning to head to Spain so she can enjoy the warmth. My focus has to be on my family and now that you have a family, that needs to be your first priority. That little girl needs you, Felix.'

Felix had frowned for a moment, his mind working fast as he'd thought through a plan. He could take a twelve-month sabbatical from his present position and spend it in a less stressful working environment while figuring out how to be a parent. It could work. 'You're sure you don't mind me going to Meeraji Lake?' he'd asked.

'Mind?' Oscar had chuckled. 'Mate, you'd be doing me a big favour.'

Oscar had told him of the tight-knit community, of the excellent day-care centre, of the doctors' residence that was only two doors down from the hospital. Everything was nice and close. Felix could spend whatever free time he had with Chloe and, when he weighed it up against his current job where he was at the hospital more often than not, it had sounded brilliant.

However, Felix also wasn't ignorant of the many dangers he would face with raising a wilful young child in such a barren environment. What if she decided to run away? She could dehydrate within a short space of time. Or what if she didn't understand that the snakes and spiders in Australia were some of the deadliest in the world? Felix shuddered at the thought, realising he'd have to keep a close eye on her. How was he supposed to do that and—?

The side doors to the hospital burst open and a gaggle of voices greeted him. Felix instantly opened his eyes and stood; the sharp action combined with the plethora of urgent chatter woke Chloe and she immediately began to cry. A paramedic stretcher was being wheeled in, the patient on the stretcher moaning and groaning with pain.

'Shh… Shh…' He started jiggling Chloe up and down while stroking her lightly on the back.

'Tori, get an IV in. Adonni, get the portable ultrasound machine into emergency room one. Pat? Patrick? Can you hear me?' The woman, a redhead with her mass of long curls pulled back into an extremely haphazard bun, continued giving rapid-fire instructions to the rest of the staff. 'Bill, get Theatre prepped.'

'You're going to do the surgery here? You don't want to transfer him to Alice?'

'There's no option but to operate. We don't want Pat to end up with peritonitis,' the redhead answered before the man she'd addressed as Bill headed off in a different direction.

Chloe started to cry louder at the ruckus around her, as though completely indignant that anyone should disturb her sleep. At the sound of the child's cries, the redhead, who was dressed in scrubs, turned to look at Felix. 'Is she all right?'

'Pardon?' he called back as the stretcher disappeared into emergency room one. The redhead was patting her supine patient's hand but called out louder to him.

'Is your daughter sick? Does she require urgent treatment?'

'Uh. No. She's uh…'

The front door to the hospital opened and in walked three men, all of them looking the worse for wear with bloodied hands, bloodied faces and sheepish grins.

'What now?' The woman glared at the three of them then pointed to the waiting area, shaking her head, the loose messy bun bobbling around on her head. 'Sit. Don't move and if you dare start to fight again in here, I'll have Henry lock all of you up for three days.'

'You can't do that,' one of the men said, his tone indignant.

'Oh, yes, I can, Bazza, so don't try me.' Her tone was determined, brooking no argument.

'Er…perhaps I can help?' Felix spoke up louder as Chloe cried louder. 'If there's somewhere I can put her down so she'll settle…' He looked around at the vacant ED treatment-room beds.

'Pardon?' The redhead quickly walked over to him. 'If you could just take a seat in the waiting room, I'll be with you as soon as I can. I have an emergency appendectomy to deal with and—'

'I'm Felix McLaren,' he interrupted and when she still looked at him with a blank expression, he added, 'The new doctor. Oscar's friend. I'm here for the next year. Ring any bells?'

Patrick's moans and groans from emergency room one were getting louder. The woman took a few steps away. 'If you know how to do an appendectomy, you can most definitely help out.'

'Then I'll help out.' Again he angled his head towards the unsettled child in his arms; her cries were slowly subsiding but he could tell that the slightest noise could set her off again. 'Here. You put Chloe down somewhere and deal with the brawlers and I'll start scrubbing.' He handed Chloe to the redhead. 'I wouldn't usually offload her like this but we don't want that appendix to perforate and, besides, Oscar told me you were great with children.'

'He did?' Staring at him with big green eyes filled with confusion and a hint of annoyance, the redhead had no option but to accept the child he was thrusting into her arms.

Felix paused for a moment and fixed her with a firm look. 'Are you Harriette or Tori?'

'Sorry?' She had to raise her voice as the child hadn't enjoyed being handed off to a stranger and was making her displeasure known.

'Who are you?' he asked, leaning in towards her so his words could be better directed towards her ear. His warm breath fanned her exposed neck and she was treated to a hint of his subtle spicy scent. It was nice. It was good. It was disconcerting. Why the action should cause a burst of goosebumps to flood down the side of the body, she had no idea. She pushed the unwanted reaction to his nearness aside and met his gaze.

'I'm…um…Harriette. Harriette Jones.'

'Harriette. Good.' He nodded and took a step away, then shook his head and pointed to the door the man called Bill had gone through. 'I'm presuming it's that way to Theatres?'

'Yes, but—' She shifted the child in her arms and started jiggling up and down in an effort to help comfort the little girl, but anything else she might have said was useless as her new colleague had disappeared through the door that led to the wards and the operating theatre.

Harriette tried not to be completely miffed at the man, at his high-handedness, at the way he'd simply abandoned his daughter to the care of a stranger and waltzed off in search of *her* operating theatre. Of all the nerve!

'Then again, Harriette…' Her little internal voice of reason spoke up. 'You did say if he could do an appendectomy you'd be grateful of his help.'

'But I hadn't expected him to actually be able to do it!' her irrational side answered. It had all happened too fast. She hadn't asked him for any identification, hadn't checked his medical credentials. He could be just anyone about to embark on a surgical operation that might affect Patrick's health.

She kept jiggling the child in her arms as her mind whirled with a thousand different thoughts at once. Oscar had called her to say his friend Felix McLaren would be arriving to locum for twelve months and Harriette had been glad of the help. She just hadn't expected to be faced with an emergency, brawling idiots, her new colleague and a crying child all at the same time.

Harriette dragged in a breath and assessed the situation as she patted the little girl on the back, doing her best to ignore the cries and figure out the triage of her patients. Bazza and his bar-room brawling mates were starting to argue again and Patrick, the town's resident and self-proclaimed hypochondriac, was moaning even louder than before. At least this time Pat's symptoms were genuine. Shifting the child to free up one hand, Harriette reached for the phone on the desk and called Henry, the town's police officer.

'Can you come and give me a hand, please?' She spoke as loudly as possible, trying to compete with the little girl with the big brown eyes and exceptionally good set of lungs. She called out to Tori, the senior nurse, who was still caring for Patrick.

'I'm just going to go to the ward,' she yelled over the din. As she headed towards the ward Harriette tried to remember what her new colleague had called the little girl. What was it? It had started with a C. Chloe? Yes, Chloe.

Harriette immediately tightened her grasp on the now squirming little girl. 'Shh, Chloe,' she tried to soothe. 'It's going to be all right.' But even as she said the words, Harriette wasn't so sure she was telling the truth. On the ward, after she'd located ward sister who had just finished cleaning up after a patient, Harriette quickly explained the situation and asked if she could leave Chloe here. The poor child was now screaming and thrashing about as though she were some feral animal and Harriette's heart went out to her. The overtired toddler had lost all sense of reason and comprehension.

'Ordinarily I'd be fine with her,' the ward sister stated, 'but I'm run off my feet.'

'Call Erica. See if she can come and take care of Chloe.'

'Good idea.' While the ward sister placed the call, Harriette took Chloe over to a spare bed and sat down with the little girl. The child scrambled from Harriette's grasp and bunched herself up near the pillows, wanting to get away from the stranger. She was still crying but, thankfully, not as bad as before, now that she wasn't being held tightly.

'My name is Harriette. I'm a doctor here.'

Chloe was breathing quickly, hiccupping a few times, and once again Harriette's heart went out to her. 'I'm so sorry, Chloe. Things are a bit crazy here at the moment but one of my friends, Erica, she's going to come and stay with you. She has puppets and colouring in and stories and all sorts of fun things for you to do while you're waiting.'

Chloe's breathing was still fast but was starting to settle as Harriette spoke.

The ward sister came over. 'Erica's on her way. I'll stay with Chloe. You go.'

'Thanks, Sarah. I appreciate it.' She stood and waved to Chloe, not taking it personally when the little girl turned her head away, not wanting to look at anyone.

Harriette headed off to first check the ED, then head to Theatres. What she hadn't expected was to walk directly into a hard male chest as she pushed open the door.

'Sorry.' They both spoke in unison. Felix was exiting as she was entering and her hands immediately came up to his chest, in a reflex action, to belatedly protect herself. His hands landed on her shoulders. Their gazes met and held for a split second and in that second the rotation of the earth seemed to slow down completely.

Harriette was even more aware of his spicy scent mixed with earthy human sweat, a scent she found very pleasing indeed. She was also aware of the warmth tingling through her fingers as they rested against his cotton shirt and the firmness of his body beneath the clothing. He wasn't wearing a tie and the top button of his shirt was undone. His neck was smooth and she watched his Adam's apple slide up and down as he swallowed. Had his shirt been like that before?

She lifted her gaze back to his, her lips parting slightly as she belatedly realised he seemed to be watching her as closely as she was watching him. Her new colleague was all male. She appreciated his help and hoped it meant Felix McLaren was a good man, because he was definitely a sexy one. She smiled nervously and immediately dropped her hands, her fingertips still tingling from the touch. Time returned to normal and Felix nodded politely at her, shoving his hands into his pockets.

'Going to the changing rooms,' he mumbled. He started to walk off when her brain clicked back into gear.

'Uh… Felix?' The sound of his name on her tongue was foreign but nice at the same time. He turned on his heel and looked at her, his brow furrowed, his gaze flicking down the corridor to where he could hear Chloe crying. 'We're going to get Erica to come and look after her. Erica runs the day-care centre and is a retired teacher.'

'Good.' He turned again, seeming not to care

that much about Chloe's needs, but perhaps his thoughts were on the surgery he was about to perform. Still, Harriette should at least get some sort of identification from him, to check he really was who he said he was.

'Felix.' She stopped him again and this time he gave her a look that said he didn't like being waylaid. 'I was…uh…' Good heavens. Why was she stuttering and finding it difficult to speak? She knew it couldn't have anything to do with the fact that her fingers were still tingling from touching his chest, nor that his face had been so incredibly close to hers, nor that his spice scent was continuing to tantalise her tired mind.

'What is it?' His tone was brisk and impatient, as though she were a first-year medical student daring to speak to the high and mighty surgeon. It was enough to snap her from the trance their accidental contact had created. Harriette squared her shoulders and lifted her chin.

'I'd like to see some identification, please. After all, you're about to operate on a patient here and quite frankly you could be any Tom, Dick or Harry who just says they're a doctor.'

His jaw clenched. 'That's ludicrous. Besides, I

thought small hospitals didn't care so much about red tape.'

'I'm not asking you to fill in a mountain of forms, Felix.' Her own exasperation was starting to rise. If he was who he said he was, why couldn't he just show her a driver's licence to put her mind at ease? And why should he make her feel guilty about protecting her patients? 'I'm asking to see some identification, which I don't think, given the circumstances, is at all unreasonable.'

Exhaling harshly, he shoved his hand into the back pocket of his trousers and pulled out his wallet, opening it to reveal his Australian driver's licence, which had his name, address and date of birth as well as a picture that most definitely matched the handsome man before her.

'Satisfied?'

'Thank you.'

'Can I go now?' He jerked his thumb over his shoulder towards the corridor where the changing rooms were situated.

She bit her tongue as a thousand answers came into her mind of where she wanted to tell him to stick his overbearing and dictatorial attitude. 'Yes. I'll be assisting you in Theatre.'

'Fine.' He rubbed a hand across his forehead, then turned on his heel and headed towards the changing rooms. Was it strange for him, to just walk into a strange hospital and then operate in a strange theatre? She knew he would have come in on the daily flight to Meeraji Lake but where had he travelled from? Had today's journey been a short hop from Darwin or Alice Springs or had he been travelling for days?

'What do you think of the new doctor?' Tori asked Harriette when she returned to the ED to assess Bazza and his brawling mates. Henry had arrived and thankfully his police presence was stopping the men from starting anything else.

So many thoughts went through her mind at Tori's question. She thought Felix was exceptionally handsome but also brisk to the point of rudeness. Of course if she'd confessed that to the nurse, who was counting down the weeks until her wedding day, Tori would have plied her with excited questions and then tried to match-make them. Why did engaged couples feel that every unattached person around them needed to be paired off?

'I don't think anything,' Harriette responded. 'Patrick's been taken to Theatre?' she asked in an effort to ensure they didn't remain on the topic of the new surgeon.

'Yes.'

'Good. If you're OK to finish cleaning and stitching the wounds of our bar-room brawlers, I'll head over there.'

'Go. I'll keep the ED under control.'

'Thanks, Tori.'

Harriette did her best to keep her thoughts one hundred percent strictly professional as she changed into theatre garb. She was also conscious that Chloe didn't seem to be screaming the hospital down any more. Clearly Erica had arrived to lend a hand, so that was another problem dealt with. 'Two down, one to go.' She left the changing rooms and headed to the anteroom, joining Felix at the scrub sink.

'What did the ultrasound show?' she asked Felix.

'Confirmed enlarged appendix.' He finished scrubbing and elbowed off the taps, grabbing a sterile towel to dry his hands. 'I'll see you in there.'

Harriette watched him with curiosity as he headed into Theatre, hands upheld, back to the swinging door in order to push it open and keep his hands sterile. He was clearly focused on what needed to happen with the operation, which was a good thing, but in some respects she'd expected him to ask about the three bar-room brawlers or at least to ask how Chloe was.

Perhaps it wasn't so strange that Felix hadn't asked about Chloe or the brawlers. Perhaps it was just Harriette's way of thinking as she'd worked the majority of her medical life in small district hospitals. She'd only done two years at a major teaching hospital and that had been enough to make her hurry back to the small country hospital that had been her refuge for so many years. A small community where she'd been able to figure out her life, to get the help she'd needed when her parents had—

'Now is not the time to think about that,' she chided herself softly as she finished scrubbing, and by the time she entered Theatre she had forced her mind not to think about the bar-room brawlers, not to think about little Chloe, not to think about the other patients who were presently undergoing treatment or recuperation in the ward. Her mind was always so busy that getting it to focus on one solitary thought really did require her concentration.

'Are you fine if I take point?' he asked as she stood on the opposite side of the table to him. Patrick was draped, prepped and sedated. Bill stood beside Felix in order to provide immediate nursing assistance and Adonni, one of the nurses who was also trained in anaesthetics, was monitoring Patrick closely. They were ready to remove the offending appendix before it perforated and caused them more problems.

'Absolutely. I'm sure Pat would be honoured to be your first surgical patient here in Meeraji Lake,' she said.

'You've got that right,' Adonni added.

'I prefer not to think of my patients by name while they're on my operating table,' Felix stated.

'Really? I've always found it helps me to concentrate better, to know that Pat needs my full attention, that I need to do my best for him. That sort of thing.'

'I do not and I'd kindly thank you to refrain from speaking in such a way because the last thing I need now is to lose my concentration.' There was a crispness to his tone that brooked no argument. Harriette glanced at Adonni, the two of them sharing a brief look before apologising.

Thankfully, the surgery went well, with no complications. Felix managed to remove the appendix before it perforated. 'At least Pa...er... the patient won't be faced with a case of peritonitis thanks to your careful and brilliant skills, Dr McLaren,' she stated as he started to close the wound. 'Has it been a while since you've removed an appendix via laparotomy rather than laparoscopically?' she asked as they finished up.

'No.' He gave Adonni the nod to reverse the anaesthetic.

'Oh. That's surprising. I thought the majority of big hospitals now only remove the appendix via—'

'What if the patient's allergic to the gas used to inflate the stomach as required for laparoscopic appendectomy?' he interrupted.

'Ah, of course. Then the patient would require a laparotomy.'

'Precisely.' Felix stepped away from the table and started to degown. Adonni began to reverse the anaesthetic and Bill gave her a nod, indicating he was ready to take over monitoring Patrick.

As they were degowning Harriette decided that even if Felix was all gruff and grumpy it was no reason for her to act in the same way. She smiled at him.

'Thank you for operating, Felix.'

Felix didn't bother to look at her and she clenched her jaw, forcing her smile to stay in place.

'Good. Now, if you wouldn't mind showing me to the doctors' residence, I'd like to get settled in.'

'Of course but uh…' She frowned and pointed in the direction of the ward. 'What about Chloe? Your daughter?'

Felix stared at her blankly for what seemed like a few long seconds. 'Yes, yes. Chloe.' He frowned as though he really had forgotten he had a child. It begged the question of what had happened to the child's mother. Had she passed away? Had they divorced? Was she due to arrive in Meeraji Lake at a later date? At any rate, it did strike Harriette as a little more than odd that he'd forgotten he had a daughter. 'Of course I have Chloe to consider but I thought it best if I could get set up at my new digs before bringing her across. If that's OK with the ward sister and…er…whoever you said was going to help look after her.'

'Erica. I'm sure it'll be fine.' Harriette pulled off her cap and tossed it into a recycle bin. 'Just let me change into a fresh pair of scrubs. Won't be a minute and I'll show you where you're staying.' She turned and spun on her heel, sprinting to the change rooms before he could say another word. Within a minute she was back before him, beckoning him to follow her.

'Feel better now?' he grumbled, as though her changing had caused him great inconvenience. 'I also need to check my bags have been sent to the residence from the airstrip. The pilot told me that he would take care of it.'

'Dale's a good lad and a good pilot. They'll be there and if they're not, we'll just chase them up. In a town this small, it shouldn't take us too long to find a few suitcases.'

'Hmm.' He frowned again, trying to control the surge of irritation and impatience coursing through him. He was beyond exhausted and all he wanted now was to find his bed and sleep, but of course he had Chloe to consider, his bags to find, a thousand things to think about before he could give in to the need to sleep. It wasn't as though he wasn't used to this sort of tiredness— he was—but travelling with a small child and dealing with her tantrums had wiped him out. Give him a hectic operating schedule any day rather than dealing with a three-year-old.

'Are you ready to head over now?'

'I'd like to change out of my scrubs.' And to have a shower and something to eat and drink, he wanted to add, but that information was irrelevant and, besides, he wasn't sure he had the reserve energy to do any of those things.

Harriette shrugged, her disposition still cheerful. Did the woman have any other setting? He wasn't sure he could work around someone who smiled too much. 'I prefer to wear them most of the time when I'm working at the hospital.' She chuckled and the tinkling sound washed over him, soothing him a little, which, he had to confess, surprised him. How could a person's laughter be relaxing? He'd certainly never felt anything like that before. He looked at her lips, her perfectly formed pink lips, which, even as she spoke, seemed to be curved upwards in a smile. 'You go change. I'll check on Chloe and let the staff know you'll be collecting her later. Meet me on the ward.'

'Fine.' He turned on his heel and went to the changing rooms, needing a bit of distance from happy Harriette. Felix resisted the urge to sit down on the chair in the changing room, knowing if he did, he'd probably fall asleep right there and then. Instead, he went through the automatic motions of changing.

He headed to the ward and found his new colleague standing at the bottom of Chloe's bed, watching the child sleep.

'She's an angel,' Harriette murmured softly.

'They managed to get her to settle again?'

She chuckled and the sound soothed the pain around his temples. He resisted the urge to massage the area with his fingertips, knowing it would alert her that he was tense. The last thing he wanted was to play twenty questions with his new colleague as to exactly why he was so tense. He hadn't realised Harriette would be so chatty, as, it seemed, were most of the staff.

Harriette pointed to where two women were chatting quietly at the nurses' station. 'Erica's a genius when it comes to children and Sarah's an excellent nurse.' The two women saw them looking and waved before resuming their conversation.

Felix had never worked in a small hospital before and the informality everyone seemed to exhibit was completely foreign to him. Still, he had to make it work. He had to try the hardest he'd ever tried in order to fit in with this community, to make these next few months full of transition and peace.

He had to get it right. In the past he'd only had himself to contend with but times had changed. He was responsible for Chloe. He was her guardian and, although he was still annoyed with his brother for doing this to him, he wasn't the type of man to shirk his responsibilities.

Chloe was an innocent little girl and as he looked down at her, her breathing peaceful and trusting, he knew he couldn't let her down. He'd

taken a risk by coming here and he was now desperate for it to pay off because if it didn't…the
consequences didn't bear reflection.

CHAPTER TWO

By THE TIME Harriette went to bed that night, it was well after midnight. Although it had been great having Felix perform Patrick's surgery, his arrival had left her feeling highly confused. It wasn't the fact that she now had to share a house with him. She'd lived in shared housing before and she'd been fine. Nor was it the fact that he had a child who would also be under the same roof. She'd lived in the same house as a child for a very long time. No, it was more to the point that her new colleague was already causing conflicting emotions within her and she wasn't at all happy about it.

This was supposed to be *her* time...the time in her life when she didn't need to worry about anyone else except herself. For so long she'd given everything she had for other people and, while she didn't regret it one little bit, she'd been holding onto the day when her time really would be her own. So the last thing she wanted was to be thinking about her new and exceedingly handsome colleague and housemate!

Naturally she appreciated his skills as a medical professional but she couldn't say she was all that impressed with his 'big city' attitude towards the patients. They were just a number to him, not people with names and families and real-life problems. She'd once been told by a big-city doctor that she was a fool to pursue surgical training for that very reason. She was too emotionally involved with her patients, she couldn't be objective, might falter and fail when it counted most because she couldn't effectively distance herself.

'The great surgeons, the truly *great* surgeons, always detach themselves from their patients. Provide first-class treatment? Of course. Be polite and understanding? Most definitely.But overly sympathetic? Empathetic? No. Not if you want to be a great surgeon.' That was what she'd been told when she'd chosen to specialise in surgery.

If Felix McLaren continued to treat every patient in Meeraji Lake with the same professional distance he'd shown to Patrick, then she feared she might have a revolt on her hands. If patients refused to see Felix because of his standoffish attitude, that would mean more patients on her own list—both clinical and surgical—and she'd still be run off her feet. If the purpose of him coming here was to lend a hand, and if he wasn't prepared to relax his usual policies regarding patient care, then he might as well leave because he wouldn't be doing anyone in the town or district any good—no matter how brilliant he was.

Harriette shook her head as she brushed her teeth. There was no room for that big-city attitude out here in the middle of the Australian outback. She would never succumb to the professional distance she'd been advised to maintain but would Felix? The main flaw with the entire argument, as far as she was concerned, was that she had no desire to become a *great* surgeon; she just wanted to save people's lives. What was so wrong with that? She wasn't interested in climbing the hospital hierarchy ladder, wasn't interested in having her accomplishments written up in medical journals. Naturally she wanted to be a *good* surgeon but having her opinion sought after by other doctors was not on her radar. Was Felix? Had he been on his way up the ladder? Sought after by his peers? If so, then why on earth had he chosen to come here?

Harriette knew she needed to put Felix and his professional behaviour out of her mind. She had more than enough to keep her thoughts occupied. At the end of this year, she would sit her final exam in general surgery and then she could continue to work in small communities like this one, to help out, to make a real difference where it was needed most.

She'd worked for so long, she'd worked so hard and she'd done it not only for herself but for Eddie. Her darling Eddie. How she loved him. Even at the thought of him, she felt a lightness start to settle over her, her shoulders relaxing. Harriette glanced over at her phone and when she'd finished brushing her teeth, she sent him a text message, knowing he'd just be starting work over in Paris. She finished her message with lots of lovehearts and smiley faces and kisses.

Feeling more calm and with thoughts of her new colleague replaced by thoughts of Eddie, she lay down in her bed, sighing with happiness when she received a reply message from Eddie, which consisted solely of emoticons of funny faces plus a love heart at the end. Her Eddie loved her and as far as she was concerned, it meant that everything was perfect with her little world. She didn't need to worry about her new colleague or his daughter. It didn't matter what sort of day she'd had at the hospital, good or bad, so long as she could rely on Eddie to always be there for her, she could cope. Harriette closed her eyes and allowed the bliss of a well-deserved sleep to settle over her.

The loud scream that pierced the air had her up and out of bed like a shot. Dressed only in a pair of cotton short pyjamas and matching T-shirt, she rushed towards where she thought the scream might have originated, her heart pounding wildly against her chest.

She heard crying, the sound of a little girl, clearly frightened. Harriette stepped into the shared lounge room of the doctors' residence and turned on the light, intending to head to the other side of the house, which was where Felix and his daughter, Chloe, had their rooms. Harriette was on one side of the house, the two of them on the other. Separate bathrooms but shared lounge, kitchen and dining rooms.

As soon as the light illuminated the room the little girl screamed once again and it was then Harriette realised the child was standing in the middle of the room, fear filling her eyes. 'Mummy! Mummy!' Her cries were becoming louder, her voice strained, her beautiful British accent conveying her distress.

'Shh, sweetie. It's all right.' She headed towards the child.

'No. No.' Chloe held up her hands towards Harriette as though fending her off. 'Leave me alone. Leave me *alone*! I *want* my *mummy*!' She actually stamped her foot and Harriette's heart melted.

'Of course you do, darling, but she's not here right now.' Harriette sat down on the floor a little way off from the child in an effort to bring herself more to Chloe's height and to hopefully not cause any more distress. 'I'm Harriette. Remember?'

'I want my mu…mu…mummy.' The words hitched in her throat and Harriette's own emotions started to be affected by Chloe's distress.

'And you're Chloe.' She knew she needed to distract the child long enough to calm her down. Even though the child didn't answer her, Harriette continued. 'That's a very pretty name. How old are you? Are you two years old?'

At this deliberate affront, Chloe's eyes cleared for a moment and she fixed Harriette with the same glare Felix had used when they'd first met. 'I'm not. I'm nearly four,' she replied with firm indignation.

'Wow. Such a big girl. I'll bet you're going to have a great birthday party, with presents and cakes.' It was clearly the wrong thing to say as the vulnerability immediately returned to Chloe's eyes, mixed with distress. 'Do you know where you are, Chloe?' Harriette asked softly, wanting to reach out to the little girl, but she knew if she did she risked alienating Chloe even further.

'Where's my mummy?' At least this time Chloe didn't scream the question but her lower lip began to wobble. 'I *want* my *mummy*!'

'I know, darling. Why don't we go and find your daddy?' And give him a dagger look for not waking up to his daughter's screams.

'Daddy?' There was a thread of hope in her

tone. If she couldn't have her mother, then her father was the next best thing.

Harriette nodded and stood, beckoning the child to follow her. She didn't make any effort to touch the girl, nor to wipe away the tears, nor hug her close, which was what she really wanted to do. The poor little angel was clearly frightened and yet her tears had started to subside at the thought of her father. Chloe was still watching Harriette cautiously but at least she'd stopped the loud screams and hysterical crying. How could Felix have slept through them? He was a surgeon. He was used to being woken up in the middle of the night, of sleeping deeply but waking quickly when an emergency arose.

'Daddy's bedroom is this way.' Harriette took slow steps towards Felix's part of the house, patiently waiting as Chloe slowly followed. 'I'm surprised he didn't wake up when he heard you crying.' In fact, she was surprised the entire town hadn't woken up as Chloe's screams had been that loud…or had they? Perhaps Chloe hadn't been crying too loudly after all and perhaps it was simply Harriette's well-honed instincts that had instantly kicked in…or the fact that she hadn't yet slipped into a deep sleep.

When she reached Felix's closed door, she listened for a moment and could hear the sounds of faint snoring on the other side. Annoyance ripped through her. Why wasn't he looking after his daughter? Wasn't he interested in her well-being? Not only was he distant with the patients, he was distant with his own daughter? The knowledge didn't endear him to her one little bit. Working alongside a man who didn't seem to have any sort of bedside manner, both in his professional and private life, would only make things more difficult.

'Let's go wake Daddy up so he can give you a cuddle and make you feel better. Yes?' She waited for Chloe's nod of approval before knocking firmly on the door and opening it.

And there he lay. Sleeping diagonally across the double bed, his hands and feet still hanging over, he was so tall. The overhead fan was whirring on low and the floral bedcovers were bunched around the centre of his body. His snoring indicated his breathing was deep and even. He was clearly in a good REM cycle and she knew, after travelling and then operating, as well as dealing with a child, it was only natural he'd be so exhausted. Still, Chloe was his daughter, not hers, and as such he should be the one to settle her down. It was the duty of a parent—no matter the circumstances.

'Felix? Felix?' She called his name as she walked closer to the bed. 'Felix? Wake up!' She turned and looked over her shoulder, surprised to find Chloe sill standing in the doorway, shaking her head vigorously from side to side.

'That's not my daddy.'

'Felix?' Harriette spoke a little louder, hearing the hysteria beginning to rise in Chloe's tone. She walked to the head of the bed and put her hand on his shoulder, surprised to find his skin quite cool. She flatly ignored the way her fingers were tingling from where they'd made contact with his flesh. Annoyed with her own reaction, she shook his arm more firmly. 'Felix. Wake up.' Her voice was insistent. 'Chloe needs you.'

'That's *not* my daddy. My daddy is called David. That's *not my daddy*!' With that, Chloe turned and ran away, her crying starting all over again.

'What?' Harriette was now thoroughly confused, so she shook Felix even harder, calling to him. 'Wake up, Felix. There's an emergency.'

As though she'd said the magic words, Felix shifted and sat up so suddenly, he fell out of the bed, knocking Harriette over in the process and landing on top of her. She felt instant pain in her back and left arm but it quickly began to subside. She dragged a breath in, belatedly realising her mistake. That thing the world did, of standing still whenever she was within close proximity to Felix, happened again and her mind seemed to be gathering as many details about the firmness of his body, of his crazy, gorgeous scent and of the way her hands felt on his smooth, bare shoulders as she tried to shift him off her.

It was ludicrous of course. There was no way she could be physically attracted to a man she wasn't even sure she liked. In fact, during their short acquaintance, Felix McLaren had annoyed her far more than any other emotion and if she was mildly attracted to him, it was simply physical. The fact that she hadn't been this close to a semi-naked man in a rather long time meant it was her libido she had to control and nothing else. Her head was far stronger than the weaknesses of her body. She could and would control herself.

'What? What? Where am I?'

'Meeraji Lake,' she squeezed out. 'Chloe. Chloe woke up. She's upset.'

'She's awake?' There was almost the sound of dread in his voice. Was he scared of his daughter? He scrambled to his feet but not before he'd accidentally head-butted Harriette in the process.

'Ow.' She rubbed her head. 'What *is* it with you?'

'Sorry. Discombobulated.' He stood and it was then she realised why all she'd been able to feel when she'd been trying to extricate herself from beneath him was hard, male flesh. Felix McLaren was dressed only in a pair of boxer shorts, his perfectly broad shoulders appearing much broader from where she sat on the floor, looking at him silhouetted against the light that was coming in from the lounge room.

Control. Self-control. That was all she needed… and not to keep staring at his gorgeous…firm… Harriette forced herself to look away and cleared her throat. So Felix was a perfect male specimen.

She'd seen several, more than several in fact, during her time. She was a doctor. She was used to seeing the male form and… Harriette tried a few deep breaths to bring herself better under control. If she didn't look at him, then that should work. Instead, she rubbed her head once more and tried to focus on what he was saying.

'Where did she go?'

'I don't know,' Harriette grumbled as she rubbed her head and slowly stood to her feet. 'She ran away, saying you weren't her daddy. Her daddy's name is David.'

'Her father's name *is* David,' Felix stated as he reached for a T-shirt and headed out towards the lounge room.

'She's probably hiding somewhere.'

'Chloe? Chloe? It's all right. I'm here to help you.'

Harriette followed him but when she reached the lounge room, it was to find no trace of the child. 'Where is she? Chloe?' she called. Felix was now starting to search behind curtains, under tables.

'Can you check your part of the house, please? She has the tendency to either hide or run away when things go wrong but thankfully, as the doors to the house are locked, she can't have got far.'

A prickle of apprehension washed over her and she slowly shook her head. 'The doors aren't locked,' Harriette stated slowly, then, as though the reality of the situation dawned clearly on both of them, she rushed into her part of her house and started to search, calling the little girl's name as she went.

'What do you mean they're not locked? Didn't you lock them when you came back from the hospital?' She could hear the censure in his tone and she didn't appreciate it one little bit. How dared he imply that this was her fault? How was she to know that Chloe had a tendency to run away? How was she to know the child would wake in the middle of the night, crying for her parents who clearly weren't anywhere to be found? And more to the point, if Felix wasn't Chloe's father, then who was he and why did he have charge of the little girl? No wonder the child was distressed.

Gritting her teeth once more, Harriette pushed the questions aside and focused on the more important task at hand—finding Chloe as quickly as possible. She checked in every small space where a child could hide, in the closets, beneath the bed, in the spare room, the bathroom— everywhere—but Chloe wasn't to be found. Harriette grabbed her mobile phone from the bedside table. If Chloe wasn't in the house, it meant she was outside and for that they would need help.

She returned to the lounge room where, for some reason, Felix was lifting the cushions on the chairs as though desperate to find Chloe beneath there. 'You haven't lost your car keys,' she stated. 'You've lost a child.'

'*I've* lost a child? How could *you* not lock the doors?' He spread his arms wide with astonishment, his voice indicating *she* was a prime imbecile for not doing such a simple, mundane task.

'We live in the middle of nowhere, Felix. Crime is basically non-existent. No one locks their doors and I had no idea Chloe was the type of child to run away!' Tensions were increasing to the point where soon they would be embroiled in a slanging match, rather than focusing on finding the girl.

As though Felix realised this as well, he rubbed

both hands over his face before pushing them through his hair, causing the follicles to stand on end, making him look vulnerable, confused and incredibly sexy. Harriette actually shook her head, pushing the thoughts away. Focus. They needed to focus.

Felix strode to the back door, which was in the kitchen, and pointed. 'Did you leave the door like this? The main door open and the screen door closed?'

'No. I shut the main door.'

'But you didn't lock it.' Again, there was that tone of his, calling her stupid without actually saying so.

Harriette didn't bother replying. Instead, she grabbed the emergency torches from the cupboard and slipped on a pair of flip-flops. 'Here. Start looking. I'll call Henry.'

'Henry?'

'The town's police officer. He can help organise a search.'

'Search?' The word stopped Felix in his tracks for a split second and Harriette saw deep fear and concern flash across his face. 'Surely we won't need to go that far? Surely you and I can find her? I mean, it's far too late to wake the entire town in order to find a stubborn three-year-old, right?'

'This is the outback, Felix. Things can turn from bad to worse in a split second.' Before he could say another word, she punched a pre-set number into her phone and put it on speaker phone.

'This is Henry,' a sleepy male voice said a moment later.

'It's Harriette, mate. The new doctor's daughter...' She paused on the word but shook her head and continued as Felix headed past her, his torch on, looking around the back of the house. There wasn't much grass, nor were there fences between the properties. 'She's upset and confused and she's gone out of the house. We're not sure where she is but she can't have gone far.'

Felix listened with half an ear as Harriette spoke to the local cop, all the while flashing his torch around the area, calling for Chloe. She really couldn't have gone too far, right? She was confused, frightened and upset as well as being forthright, determined and stubborn. The problem was he had no idea what was going through her head and even if he hadn't been still groggy from jet lag, he still wouldn't have been able to predict where she might go. He felt so helpless. He didn't know Chloe. She didn't know him. It was why he'd come here in the first place, to try and be a father to the little girl, but as he had no idea how to be a father and as she clearly didn't want him in the role it was making life incredibly complicated.

He knew it wasn't Harriette's fault the door hadn't been locked. She was right. How was she to know that Chloe had a tendency to run off? Felix closed his eyes for a brief second and rubbed a hand across his temples. He was exhausted, jet-lagged, running on the last shred of his energy reserves and he honestly didn't know how much longer he'd last.

'You'll continue until you find her,' he told himself sternly. Chloe was his responsibility and he knew—or at least he hoped—that within the next few months they'd be able to find a footing where they could both appreciate the situation they were in and make the best of it. He did care for the child. He had a familial love for her and it was that that had spurred him forward to become her legal guardian. His heart ached for the pain and confusion she must be feeling.

'Chloe?' He called her name as he checked behind a native shrub. He didn't call too loudly as he didn't want to wake people up, nor scare the child.

'Chloe?' Harriette yelled as she came out of the house, her voice booming in the dark.

'Shh. She can't have gone far,' Felix said, feeling self-conscious and worried and confused and completely out of his depth.

'She won't hear me if I don't yell and you're wrong that she couldn't have gone far. When a three-year-old decides to run, their little legs can be pretty fast.'

'Even if she does hear you,' Felix hissed, keeping his curt words low, 'she still might not answer.'

Harriette ignored him and shone her torch around the area, looking down the path that led to the clinic and the hospital. 'There's no point in arguing semantics, Felix. Where do you think she might have gone? Maybe she went back to the hospital? After all, there are lights to pave the way and she might have just followed them, still unsure where they led.'

'I don't know.'

'Chloe!' she yelled again and listened for a response but nothing came. 'You don't have a clue what she might do?'

'No.'

'How often has she run away like this before?'

'Twice.'

She gritted her teeth, knowing he should have taken better precautions to ensure Chloe's safety, but what mattered now was finding Chloe before something else did. There were plenty of four legged predators out at night as well as snakes. True, they usually didn't come this close to the town but there were always exceptions. Harriette hoped tonight wasn't one of them.

'I'll check the hospital. You check down the path that leads to the retirement village and community centre.' Harriette shone her torch in the direction he should go. 'Have you got your mobile phone with you?'

'No. It's inside. I'll do a double-check in there again in case we missed a hiding spot and pick it up. Then I'll head to the retirement village.' He spoke the words as though he was getting things clear in his head, as though he really wasn't capable of coherent thought right now and was happy she was making the plans.

'Good. Call me if you find her.' Harriette headed off down the path towards the clinic and the hospital.

'Wait. I don't know your number.'

'Ask anyone you meet. They all have it,' she called, before disappearing around the side of the house and out of his view. Felix frowned as he headed back into the house, grumbling to himself.

'What if I don't meet anyone? They're all asleep so what am I supposed to do—?' A sound stopped him and he paused, then said clearly and firmly, 'Chloe, if you're hiding in here, you need to come out immediately. You're starting to worry me…and soon, there will be lots of people trying to find you and really, well, we all just want to know you're safe.' And he did. He wanted to know he hadn't failed his brother by not being a good enough guardian.

Nothing else seemed to matter now. The past was the past and even though he and David had managed to patch things up a few years ago, they still hadn't spoken much. The best thing he could do for his brother now was to care for Chloe. *That* was how he would make peace with the pain piercing his heart. Chloe had to come first.

'Chloe?' He called her name everywhere he went as he rechecked every nook and cranny in the house, including Harriette's side. The little girl really wasn't anywhere to be found. He picked up his phone, slipped on his Italian loafers, then headed on the path towards the Meeraji Lake retirement village and community hall.

Surprisingly, as he drew nearer to the community hall, he was astonished to find quite a few people coming out, many of them retirees, laughing and joking together.

'What are you all doing out so late?' he asked, switching off his torch, the light outside the community centre casting enough light for him to see their faces.

'Who are you?' one of them asked.

'Dr McLaren. Oscar Price's friend.'

'And what might *you* be doing up so late and dressed as such?' one of the ladies asked, waggling an arthritic finger at him and giggling.

Felix looked down at his attire of T-shirt, boxer shorts and loafers. Clearly this wasn't how he'd wanted to meet the townsfolk but there was nothing he could do about that now.

'My…er…child—Chloe. She's three, nearly four. She's run away.'

'Why didn't you say so first off?'

'Has Henry been called?'

'Where's Harriette? Does she know?'

'How long ago? Are we talking hours or minutes?'

'Er…' He tried to compute all the questions that were spoken in unison. 'Only a few minutes ago. Five. Maybe five minutes by now. Harriette's checking the clinic and hospital. Henry's been called.'

'Good thing the council meeting ran rather late tonight,' one of the men said. 'What did you say her name was?'

'Chloe. She's almost four years old.' And just like that, they all started helping. No other questions, no forms of censure. Nothing. Some of them switched on their mobile phones, using them to light the way, others started calling more people to come and join the search. They were a community. They cared. They had no idea who he was, they hadn't even met Chloe and yet here they were, immediately offering assistance. Felix was…humbled as well as appreciative.

'Chloe? Chloe?' They all started calling and spread out, helping him to look for her. Felix hoped the child wasn't in any danger. She couldn't be, could she? The poor thing had already been through enough in her short life. She didn't need more. The concern he'd felt earlier doubled as five minutes turned into ten.

Henry was now on the scene and Harriette had checked the clinic and the hospital, alerting the night staff of the situation.

'It's all right, Felix. We'll find her,' Harriette reassured him after she'd spoken to the people who were awake and helping them search. He'd also lost count of the number of times people had asked him where he thought Chloe might have gone and his helplessness increased when he simply had to shrug and say he had no idea.

'The next step is to raise the alarm and wake the volunteer firefighters so we can get some big lamps set up and cars heading up and down the main roads with their spotlights,' Henry said.

Felix sat down in the gutter outside the hospital and put his head in his hands. How had this happened? He clearly wasn't fit to be a parent to the child. Surely tonight proved that.

'We'll find her,' Harriette said again as she sat down next to him and put her hand on his shoulder.

'I can't do this. I can't.'

'If you need to go back to the house, that's fine. We all understand. We'll get the search party organised and—'

'I meant I'm not cut out to be a parent.'

Harriette processed his words for a moment before asking softly, 'Who's David?'

'My brother.'

'So...Chloe's your *niece*?'

'Yes, and until my brother and his wife were killed in a car accident four months ago I had no idea I was listed as her guardian.'

'Chloe's parents have passed away?' Harriette's words were filled with sadness and compassion.

'Yes.'

'And you're her guardian?'

'Yes, but I—' He stopped and shook his head. Around them people were talking and organising and planning. He felt incredibly helpless. 'I don't know how to be a parent.' He hung his head after speaking the words out loud. 'Clearly I'm no good. I didn't even realise she was upset and then I didn't check the doors were locked and she hates me and she cried almost the entire time on the plane—and it's a long flight from England to Australia and—' He buried his face in his hands, his tone filled with anguish. 'I have no idea what to do. I don't know. I just don't know. And now she's lost. Lost in a strange place. Not knowing anything or anyone and…oh, Harriette…she must be *so* frightened.'

Harriette listened to him, her heart going out to him and the little girl who had been orphaned. She had many questions but now was not the time. What Felix needed right now was reassurance. Time was ticking by and although it felt as though hours had passed since they'd started to search, that wasn't the case at all.

Harriette sniffed and cleared her throat and when Felix turned to glance at her, he could see a tear sliding down her cheek, the light from the street light above making it glint in the darkness. 'We'll find her, Felix.' She took a deep, cleansing breath, her words now filled with determination. 'We're a strong community and when something like this happens, we all band together, leaving no stone unturned. We support and—'

'Found her!' came a loud female call from the very far end of the street.

'What?' Felix was on his feet like a shot and Harriette wasn't far behind him. They sprinted towards where the woman's voice had come from and, in the dim lights from around them, they saw a woman coming towards them, carrying a small child in her arms.

'Oh, Erica. You absolute legend.'

When Erica reached Felix, he immediately took Chloe from her and hugged the child close.

'Where was she?' Harriette asked.

'At the bus stop. Waiting.'

'Oh, the poor love. The bus stop is quite a way from the house but clearly she was determined to get out of here.'

'Chloe. Chloe, you had me scared out of my wits.' Felix's words were soft and filled with emotion. He tried to ease her head back but she'd buried it in his neck, her little arms holding him tight. 'I was so worried about you.' He sniffed, exhaustion, stress and relief all mixing together.

Chloe pulled back a little and looked at his cheek, lifting her chubby hand to wipe at the tears. 'You're crying?'

'Because I'm so relieved you're OK. I need you to be safe, Chloe. I need to know where you are. I need to keep you *safe*,' he reiterated.

'Why?' the child asked softly and Harriette found herself holding her breath.

'Because we're family,' he returned and the answer seemed to settle the child somewhat. 'Let's get you home,' he said.

'To England?' she asked with hope.

'Just back to our new house.'

'With Harriette?' Chloe asked.

And it was as though Felix had even forgotten his new colleague was there because he shifted the child in his arms so he could look at his housemate. 'Yes, Harriette lives there, too.'

'I want to sleep with Harriette,' the child declared and held out her hands towards Harriette, lunging so quickly, Felix had no option but to let her go. 'I want to sleep with you. I used to sleep with Mummy when I had bad dreams.'

'I think you need to get used to sleeping in your own bed,' Felix started, but before he could say another word, Harriette interjected.

'Of course you can sleep in my bed,' Harriette said as they started walking back, most of the searchers now having been told that the child had been found safe and well. Felix shook hands with everyone but the women were having none of this hand-shaking business and pulled Felix close for a hug. Harriette had to smile at the look of shock and confusion on his face. Confusion at what? At being so warmly and readily accepted by the community? This same community he'd previously been determined to keep at arm's length? Soon he would realise that in a district this small, it was inevitable to make relationships with the people who were also your patients. There were no case-file numbers here. There were only people, people who needed a holistic approach to medicine and that involved having relationships with them.

Erica, the woman who had looked after Chloe while they'd been operating on Patrick, the woman who had eventually found Chloe at the bus stop, gave Felix a big, warm hug.

'You bring her to see me at the day-care centre tomorrow. We need to get Chloe mixing with other children in the district, to let her know she has friends here so that she feels secure and loved,' Erica told him, and Felix nodded in agreement.

'I'm just so glad she was found and that she's OK,' he said quite a while later as he stood beside Harriette's bed. Chloe was lying snuggled next to Harriette, sound asleep. 'She *is* OK, isn't she?'

'She's a little shaken but that's to be expected. Psychologically, I think tonight pales in comparison with what she's already been through.'

'I'll say.' He walked over to pick her up.

'What are you doing?'

'I'm putting her into her own bed.'

'Why?'

'Because she's asleep now and all the parenting books say that the children will only learn to sleep in their own beds if they sleep there every night, regardless of where they may have fallen asleep.'

'Oh, hang the parenting books.' Harriette shook her head and placed a protective arm over Chloe's little body. 'She's fine where she is. You go and get some sleep. We'll be fine.'

'Hang the parenting books? How can you say that?'

'Because I know more about parenting than any parenting book, mate.'

'You do? Do you have kids?'

Harriette fixed the covers over Chloe before turning out the bedside light. 'Make sure the doors are locked before you turn in. Thanks, Felix,' she said, smothering a yawn.

And just like that, he was dismissed.

CHAPTER THREE

THREE DAYS. FELIX had been in Meeraji Lake for three days and it seemed as though Chloe preferred Harriette to him. In fact, Chloe seemed to prefer anyone to him. She'd willingly gone to the day care that was run by Erica; she'd willingly played with other children at day care; she'd gleefully told him in that posh little voice of hers that she liked *all* of them better than she liked him. Yesterday, after day care, he'd been running late in the ED and so Tori had taken Chloe around to the ward so she could visit with some of the patients. When Felix had finished his work, he'd headed to the ward to find Chloe sitting at the end of Patrick's bed, chatting with him and laughing and entertaining all the other patients on the ward.

The child simply preferred anyone and everyone to him. It was as though she was trying to punish him in some way, showing him that she was more than capable of loving, of showing affection, but that she simply *chose* not to show any to him—the man who was her guardian. He knew logically that, deep down inside, she didn't mean it. She was hurting and she was taking it out on him but, illogically, he couldn't help but be hurt by the little girl's actions.

Instead of doing the sensible thing and talking to someone about it, Felix quashed all the emotions he was feeling way down deep and focused on his job. He was getting to know the Meeraji Lake protocols, getting to know the patients who seemed to drive for miles just for a check-up. He realised Harriette, who seemed to always be happy and jovial and willing to listen to anyone who was talking, might have had a point—that here in such a small and intimate community, patients were people, not just a diagnosis.

That morning, as he and Harriette sat at the table having cereal for breakfast, he discovered the reason why the hospital ED had been vacant when he'd arrived in the town three days ago. Apparently, Patrick had collapsed at the community centre and, rather than sending an ambulance, it had been easier to just take a barouche down to the community centre, treat Patrick and then wheel him back. The ward sister had been in charge of the hospital, but at the time he'd walked into the ED she'd been caring for a patient who had just been ill all over the ward floor.

'It happens,' Harriette said after explaining the situation to him. 'When it doesn't rain it pours. All the drugs are securely locked up as well as any patient information. Plus we're fortunate that the nursing staff are happy to rotate through the different positions as well as using their special-ist skills when needed.'

'I don't follow.'

'Well Sarah is a trained midwife, Adonni is trained as in anaesthetics and Bill holds quali-fications in geriatric nursing. Tori's trained in emergency nursing and is also hospital adminis-trator so she's the one who does a lot of the paper work. They're our full-time nurses and then they all rotate throughout the other positions of work-ing in the ED or theatres or being ward sister or doing immunisation clinics. It's a very different system to a large hospital but it seems to work.'

'And what if there are emergencies? Four nurses

and two doctors surely isn't enough to handle a big emergency?'

'There are quite a few trained part-time nurses in the district so they come in to cover leave and days off or when there's a big emergency."

'You sound as though you've been working here for quite a while yet I could have sworn when I met with Oscar he said you were covering for them while he and Daisy were looking after her mother.'

'I am. I've been here a total of almost ten weeks.'

'That's not long.'

She shrugged and poured herself a glass of iced tea. 'Is that a problem?'

'No. No. It's just that you seem so…integrated into small-town life.' He frowned, not sure he was making much sense. 'What I mean is—'

'I know what you mean,' she interrupted. 'Perhaps I'm simply brilliant in any environment?' She looked at him over the rim of her glass as she took a sip.

'Perhaps.' He said the word slowly, as though he wasn't quite sure of her mood. Was she teasing him? Was she being serious? Was she fishing for compliments?

'Or…perhaps I'm related to half the people in this town, which means it's easier for me to…integrate.' She raised one eyebrow at him, which only made him lower two of his into a confused frown. He simply didn't know Harriette well enough to know when she was teasing or when she was being serious. He decided to remain cautious as, right now, anything and everything she was saying might be true.

'Perhaps,' he repeated.

'Or…' As she drawled the word she raised the glass to her lips and, although she was talking, he found he was completely captivated by her actions. He was all too aware of the way her perfectly formed lips parted to accept the cool liquid, her perfectly smooth neck as she swallowed, the tip of her pink tongue sliding out to lick her lower lip as though eager to retain every drop of the delicious iced tea. Felix drew in a deep breath, forcing himself to look away, to focus on what she was saying.

This wasn't how he treated female colleagues. He didn't ogle them. He didn't stare at them in an impolite manner. He respected them. He admired all his colleagues, regardless of gender, for their intelligence and abilities, and during the past three days he'd come to admire Harriette— her ease and friendliness with the patients as well as her professionalism.

It was true that on a physical level he found her attractive, especially with the way her beautiful auburn locks seemed to have a mind of their own, never allowing themselves to be tamed into the hairstyle she chose. Or the way her green eyes seemed to sparkle with emotion, whether it was anger, annoyance or mirth…as was being displayed at the moment. She was teasing him and he liked it, even though he couldn't remember what it was she'd just said.

'Felix?' She was looking cautiously at him now, a slight furrow of concern creasing her brow. 'Earth to Felix?' She snapped her fingers in his direction in order to get his attention. When he met her gaze, she smiled. 'Are you all right?'

'Yes. Sorry. Too many things on my mind. So you're not related to half of the town?'

'No.' He could see the twinkle in her eyes, the corners of her mouth curving upwards.

'Just a small girl from a small town. Big cities give me the heebie-jeebies so when I was asked to come and help out, I was more than happy to transfer from Melbourne city to outback Australia.'

'Where did you say you grew up?'

She shrugged and took another sip from her glass before standing and walking over to the kitchen bench, needing a bit of distance from him, especially if she was going to successfully avoid talking about herself. 'Small towns in South Australia and Victoria. We…uh…I moved around a bit.' This was no time for her to launch into an explanation of just why she'd ended up in small towns, or why she'd moved so often. Even though her situation was more acceptable nowadays, she still didn't like to discuss it with someone until she knew them much better.

'So I guess that explains why I can be here for six weeks and appear as though I belong. I'm used to tight-knit communities. I'm used to not locking my doors at night. I'm used to seeing my patients as people, rather than just another case-file number.' She leaned against the kitchen bench and sipped her tea, watching him closely.

'You're such a big-town man, Felix. That was evident from the first time I saw you.'

'You make it sound like that's a bad thing?' He finished drinking his coffee, then stood and started clearing the table, not just his own dishes but hers as well. She appreciated that. Chloe hadn't wanted to eat anything other than a banana and was presently supposed to be in her room putting her shoes on. The little girl clearly knew her own mind and Harriette couldn't help but smile at the long road ahead that Felix would need to navigate.

'Not at all.' She finished her drink, adding it to the pile of dirty dishes in the dishwasher. 'All I'm saying is that I can understand why it might take you a while to settle in here.' She checked the digital clock on the microwave and grimaced. 'We're going to be late. You'd better get Chloe to day care or you'll be late for clinic.' Harriette picked up her sunhat and bag before heading towards the door.

'Can't you take her?' Felix called. 'She hates me.'

Harriette's answer was a chuckle. 'She doesn't

hate you, Felix. She's been through so much pain, and seeing you reminds her of that.'

'Is that why she's friendly and happy with everyone else in the town except me?'

Harriette nodded. 'She's just behaving the way she's behaving because that's how she behaves. She's three years old.'

'Well, there's sound logic for you,' he replied with a snort of derision. 'What am I supposed to do?' Even he could hear the desperation in his tone.

Harriette smiled warmly at him and once again Felix felt that tightening in his gut. She had a lovely smile. 'Just be there for her. She'll come around.'

'When?'

'When you stop reminding her of her father. Thankfully, she's almost four and it's very rare children have crystal-clear memories from a time before they start pre-school. She'll settle down.'

'I don't want her to forget her father, or her mother for that matter.'

'Of course not. That's not what I'm saying.' Harriette angled her head to the side, a few tendrils falling loose from the messy half-bun she'd wound it into. She stared at him for a long moment, long enough that it made him feel a little self-conscious. 'Did you and David look alike?'

'A bit. Same height. Same dark hair, brown eyes.'

'That's what I mean. You *remind* her of her father but you're not him. That's got to be confusing for her. Just wait it out.'

'That's it?' He spread his arms wide. 'That's your advice? Wait it out?'

Harriette laughed, the sweet tinkling sound washing over him and having a strange calming effect on him at the same time. He cleared his throat, unable to look away from the alluring image of the woman before him. 'Just love her, Felix. It isn't that hard to do. She's a gorgeous girl.'

'For you, maybe.'

Harriette laughed again, the sound following her as she put her hat on and left the house.

Love her? That thought stayed with him for the rest of the day. Sitting in the ED later that afternoon, he looked blankly at the paperwork he was supposed to be filling in, not at all sure how he was supposed to *just love* Chloe. When he took

her to day care in the mornings, it was like pulling teeth to get her to wear her hat, something it
was necessary for her to do in such an incredibly
hot climate. When it was nighttime, she seemed
to hate every food there was and preferred to eat
a banana or a cheese sandwich. In fact, yesterday all she'd eaten for breakfast, lunch and dinner had been a cheese sandwich. He'd made her
a bowl of cereal. She'd thrown a tantrum. He'd
made her some toast. Another tantrum and not
just stamping her foot and being defiant, but a
full-on yelling, screaming match that had had
him throwing up his hands in despair and going
to his room.

When he'd come out, it had been to find her
sitting at the table, quietly eating a cheese sandwich that Harriette had made for her.

'You gave in to her?' he'd questioned and received such a death stare from his new colleague,
he'd immediately backed off.

Felix leaned his head back and shut his eyes.
What was he doing here? He'd brought a child he
didn't know to the middle of nowhere and now
was being ostracised by said child for bringing
her to the middle of nowhere! How could a three-

year-old possibly understand the ramifications of what was happening? How could she possibly make him feel so guilty for trying to do what he thought was best for her? What had made him think he could be a parent? He'd never wanted to have children. His own childhood had seen to that and now he was stuck with a recalcitrant three-year-old who was running rings around him.

What Felix *had* wanted was to climb the hospital ladder, to be well published, have the respect of his peers, to become an incredible surgeon. He'd wanted to make an important discovery, to have accolades and awards lavished upon him and he'd been doing very well heading towards that goal before David had died and changed his destiny. Felix groaned and shook his head, looking unseeingly at the paperwork before him. He shouldn't have any ill feelings towards his brother. David clearly hadn't planned to die in a car accident.

'That's a firm look of consternation you've got going on there,' Harriette said as she came and sat down next to him, dumping a load of case notes onto the desk.

'Pardon?' He looked at her unseeingly for a moment, not having fully computed what she'd said.

'You look deep in thought.'

'I am.'

'About...' She paused and checked the case notes he was writing up. 'Mrs Donovan or about Chloe?'

Felix sighed and quickly added a few words to Mrs Donovan's notes before signing his name and closing the file. 'Mrs Donovan's concern over her heart palpitations and her need for further investigation in the clinic are indeed concerning but not my most pressing concern at the moment.'

'So... Chloe?'

Felix leaned back in his chair, turning the pen over and over in his fingers. 'I can't figure out why my brother even named me as guardian. You see, David was six years younger than me and after our mother's death...' He paused. 'Well...I was at medical school, David lived at home with our dad and...' He stopped again and shook his head. 'We didn't talk for a long time. It wasn't until after he married Susan that we finally connected again.'

Harriette angled her chair towards him, giving

him her full attention. The ED was quiet for the moment so if Felix wanted to get a few things off his chest, she was more than happy to listen. She remained silent, not wanting to interrupt his train of thought. He seemed to be speaking as though it was necessary for him to get his thoughts out of his head, needing to vent, needing to try and make sense of why he'd been made guardian of his niece. He looked unseeingly at the pile of case notes before him.

'I guess, as Susan didn't have any family, I was the logical choice. I'm Chloe's biological uncle.' He heaved a sigh. 'I was working overseas in Tarparnii. It took the solicitors weeks to track me down, to let me know of the accident.'

'Where was Chloe during this time?' She couldn't help the question and when he raised his gaze to meet hers, she wondered if he'd stop confiding in her. He looked at her for a long moment before answering.

'With a foster family.' He tossed the pen onto the desk and stood, raking both hands through his hair. 'It was a short-term thing but she seemed happy there. Then I arrived, the uncle she'd never met, and her life changed again…and she hates me for it.'

'She doesn't hate you,' Harriette reiterated yet again.

'Oh, really.' Felix crossed his arms over his chest in a defensive gesture and glared at her. 'She's told me so. Right to my face. I. Don't. Like. You.'

'She's three years old! It's what three-year-olds do and I'll bet you any money she used to be just as vehement with her own parents. She's a smart little cookie but she's also only three years old.'

'Almost four,' he corrected and rolled his eyes. 'She likes *you* to take her to day care. She likes *you* to sleep with at night.'

'You can have her sleep in your bed if you like.' Her words were wry and filled with humour. 'She kicked me three times last night and she hogs all the covers.' Harriette emphasised the point by rubbing her lower back.

'And more to the point, she should be sleeping in her own bed. She should be eating a healthier diet rather than cheese sandwiches for breakfast, lunch and dinner with the occasional banana thrown in for good measure. She should know that she can't throw a tantrum anytime she doesn't get her own way and giving into those tantrums and doing what she wants isn't going to help her out in the future.'

Harriette spread her arms wide. 'For heaven's sake, Felix, cut the kid some slack. Her parents have died. She's been brought halfway around the world to a different country. The climate is different and she's not used to wearing a hat every time she goes outside. The first time she gets sunburnt, she'll learn that lesson for herself. And the fact that she's eating the same thing day in, day out, isn't bad because at least she's eating and trying to establish some sort of normalcy for herself. A cheese sandwich isn't going to let her down, isn't going to leave her. It's going to taste delicious and make her feel happy. What's so wrong with that?

'And she may not be sleeping in her own bed but at least she's sleeping. Her jet lag seems to have gone, which is more than I can say for yours, and she won't be sleeping in my bed forever, just for now. Chloe's not sick—that's a good thing. She's eating, she's sleeping, she's physically healthy. Psychologically, that little girl has been put through the wringer and the last thing she needs right now are a bunch of rules and regulations which really only exist to make *your* life easier.' She paused for a breath. 'Ditch the parenting books and go with your instinct and common sense.'

'Are you equating me with common sense?' He tried to joke but it came out flat.

'Yes, I am. I mean, you're what…in your early forties?'

'Forty-one, yes. What's your point?'

'Don't you want to have children of your own? I know it's different for men, you don't have biological clocks ticking, but surely you've thought about having children at some point in your life, right?'

'No.'

She frowned at him. 'What do you mean, "no"? You didn't want to have children or you just haven't met the right woman to have the children with?'

'I met the right woman. We married. We fought. We divorced. I devoted myself to my career.'

'And then your little brother ruins your plans by saddling you with a child.' He frowned at her words but didn't comment because the expression on his face indicated she'd hit the nail on the head. 'You don't have to feel guilty for feeling that way. Life is what it is, Felix, believe me, I know. I had loads of plans for my life but then things change. However, the one thing I've discovered is that those changed plans, the plans you hadn't even considered, sometimes turn out to be the best thing that ever happened to you.'

'Something happened to you?'

'"Something" happens to everyone. Mrs Donovan didn't expect to come to the ED today with heart palpitations. Patrick didn't expect his appendix to attack him. Oscar didn't expect to fall in love with Daisy. You didn't expect your brother to die and leave you as sole guardian of his three-year-old daughter.'

'Almost four,' he murmured softly, mimicking Chloe's words every time someone mentioned her age. It was as though she was desperate to turn four, that when she was four things would be better. Felix wasn't about to squash that feeling and fervently prayed the little girl was right.

'Don't blame your brother for doing what he thought was the right thing. He probably never thought he'd die so soon after becoming a father. The fact that he chose you means he thought you could handle it.'

'Boy, was he wrong.'

'But you *are* handling it. Don't you see?' She sighed and shook her head as though she wasn't sure what else she could say to convince him. The phone rang and she immediately reached out a hand to answer it. 'ED, Harriette speaking.' She listened, then picked up a pen and started scribbling down some notes. 'What time is the plane due to land?' She glanced up at the clock on the wall. 'That's in ten minutes.' She listened again. 'Yes. OK. We'll come down to the airstrip and meet the plane.' She put the phone down and stood.

'Apparently a patient on the daily plane to Meeraji Lake has taken ill. The pilot radioed in and said the passenger's been vomiting and it appears to be more than just airsickness. The patient has a temperature and is sweating, complaining of pains in their abdomen.'

'Doesn't sound good. What's the protocol?'

'Usually we'd get into retrieval gear but the airstrip isn't far and we don't have a lot of time. The best thing to do is to drive the ambulance down and deal with whatever we find on the spot, stabilise the patient and then bring them back here. I'll let Tori know to cover the ED while we're gone and get Bill to prep the operating theatre just in case.'

'Where is Tori?'

'In clinic giving immunisations but that can all wait for now.' While she'd been talking Harriette had located the keys to the ambulance, which was always stocked and ready for any type of emergency, and slipped on her sunglasses. She quickly made calls to the relevant people, also letting the ward sister know that until Tori arrived, the ED was unmanned.

It wasn't until they were in the ambulance that Felix hit her with the question she'd always hated, always done her best to dodge, and today was no exception.

'So…what about you? Have you ever tried the married-with-children thing?'

'Does it matter?' she asked, trying to keep her words light and impersonal.

'Er…no.' Felix frowned, surprised at her reticence to talk. 'It's just you seem to know a lot about parenting.'

'I've done quite a bit of paediatric work in the past.'

'I didn't mean to pry. I just thought we were getting to know each other a bit better. I mean, you just asked if I was married—'

'No. I asked if you'd thought of having children. *You* were the one who volunteered the information about being divorced.'

'Then you're not married?' he guessed.

'What brings you to that conclusion?'

Why was she being so cagey? It only intrigued him even more, making Harriette more of an enigma than he'd first realised. What was her story? Why had she lived in a lot of small towns? Why did she hate big cities? Why was she always so incredibly happy and optimistic? Was she hiding something? Plus, when they'd been talking about her living in small towns, she'd used 'we', then changed it to 'I'. What was she hiding?

'The fact that most women, when asked if they're married, usually say yes if they are but try and dance around the question if they're not. Now you'll probably give me some information about how you don't need marriage to define you, that you're an independent woman, that you're more than happy with your life the way it is—'

'I *am* happy with my life the way it is and I'll have you know that I've worked very hard for it to become that way. At the end of this year, I'll sit my final exams and then I'll be a qualified surgeon.'

'You're still a registrar?' he queried, clearly more surprised at this news than discovering she wasn't married. 'I didn't realise.'

'And besides, just because I may not be married, it doesn't mean I don't have a special someone in my life whom I love and adore.'

'Oh, so there *is* someone.'

'Of course there's someone. Everyone needs a special someone.'

'Where is this mysterious "someone"?' He thought for a moment. 'Is it Henry? The police officer? You two seem quite easygoing with each other.'

'Henry is married, to Sarah, one of our midwives.'

'OK, so who do you text all the time? Who texts you back?'

'You've been watching me?'

'I live in the same house as you, Harriette. Sometimes it's difficult not to notice the way you get a text, then smile that cute little smile of yours.'

Harriette raised an eyebrow and glanced over at him. 'Cute little smile?' She smirked at his words then shook her head and concentrated on getting to the airstrip. Felix thought her smile was cute? That was nice and the knowledge warmed her although she wasn't entirely sure why.

'You know what I mean.' He seemed embarrassed.

'Uh, not really but…whatever.' She slowed down to turn the corner into the entrance to the airstrip. She brought the ambulance to a halt, as close as she could to the airstrip. The plane's wheels had just touched the ground and Harriette jumped from the vehicle, immediately swatting flies as she went. 'Let's see what we're dealing with.' She opened the back of the ambulance and took out one of the emergency backpacks. She handed it to Felix, who slung it over his shoulder, then she pulled out two pairs of gloves. 'Here you go.'

It wasn't too much longer until the plane stopped and another moment more before the steps were lowered. They both headed over, pulling on the gloves so they were ready for action. Harriette was about to head up the steps in order to check on the patient, but before she had one foot on the bottom step a tall, handsome young man came bounding out of the plane.

'Surprise!' he called and opened his arms wide. In another second, he'd barrelled down the stairs and scooped Harriette up into his arms, spinning her around.

'Eddie!' She wrapped her arms around him and gave him an enormous kiss.

Felix watched, taken aback by this turn of events. Here they'd just been talking about Harriette's special someone and, clearly, the man who was holding her close, who was kissing her cheek, who was laughing at her surprise was Harriette's special *someone*.

Why he felt a thread of annoyance surge through him, Felix had no clue. No clue whatsoever.

CHAPTER FOUR

SHE HUGGED EDDIE close and kissed his face several times, clearly so incredibly happy. Felix looked away from the radiance of her smile, the way her beautiful red hair started to come loose from the haphazard bun, her tinkling laughter filtering through the air as though she had not a care in the world.

'What are you doing here?'

'I thought I'd surprise you,' the young man replied, his voice deep. In Felix's opinion, this Eddie person really did have a baby face and he couldn't help but notice that Harriette seemed quite a bit older than the man she had her arms wrapped around. Perhaps Eddie was older than he looked. Perhaps Harriette was younger than she looked, although, as he knew, she was finishing up her surgical training. That meant she had to at least be in her early thirties.

Well, some men preferred older women and

some women preferred younger men. Who was he to judge? What he was more concerned with, and what Harriette seemed to have clearly forgotten in light of her surprise visitor, was the sick patient still on board the aeroplane. Felix edged past the happily reuniting couple, determined not to give them a second thought, and walked up the steps of the plane, peering inside.

'There's no one here,' he stated, looking over at the pilot in complete confusion.

'That's right. There's no emergency.' Dale, the pilot, finished filling in his logbooks and gathered his headphones and other bits of paraphernalia so he could disembark. He grinned at Felix. 'Eddie wanted to surprise Harriette so we decided to get her to the airstrip under false pretences.'

'You *faked* an emergency?' There was disbelief and censure in Felix's tone. 'You took the only two doctors in town away from the hospital's emergency department, which therefore required our senior nurse to leave the immunisation clinic in order to staff the now vacant ED, and you thought this was a good idea?'

The young pilot had the grace to look guilty at Felix's words. 'We didn't think—'

'No. Clearly you did not. What if there had been a real emergency, an emergency which required the ambulance and the attention of the doctors?'

'Was there?'

Felix paused for a moment before reluctantly admitting, 'No. But there might have been,' he added quickly. 'Emergency service call-outs aren't some sort of joke, young man.' With that, Felix exited the aeroplane, stalking briskly to where Harriette was now loading Eddie's duffel bag into the front seat of the ambulance.

'You can ride in the back,' she told him, her smile still wide and happy. 'But don't touch anything.' She waggled a finger at him, then stared at him a moment longer as though she really couldn't believe he was standing in front of her. 'Put your seatbelt on,' she remarked as she took the backpack from Felix and stowed it back in place. She shut the rear doors of the ambulance and went around to the driver's side.

'That's it?' Felix asked. 'Put your seatbelt on?'

'What?' She waved goodbye to Dale, then looked across at Felix. 'What's wrong?'

He looked into her face and his breath caught in his throat. He'd known she was an attractive woman but right now, the way she looked so incredibly happy, as though she could take on the world and knew she would win, brought out her inner radiance. She was…stunning.

'Uh…' Felix tried to think of what he'd been saying but his mind was blank.

'Are you ready to go?' she asked as she climbed into the ambulance. 'We should get back to the hospital asap and let Tori know it was a false alarm.'

As he walked around to the passenger side his brain seemed to click back into gear. 'They could be charged,' he remarked softly while he put his seatbelt on.

'Who?'

Felix glanced back towards where Eddie was sitting.

'Eddie and Dale?'

'Yes. They've radioed in a false emergency, removing valuable resources which may have been needed elsewhere.'

'But we weren't. We'll be back at the hospital in a few minutes and everything will be back to normal. Henry won't charge them.'

'Won't he?'

'No. He and Eddie get along really well.'

Felix frowned. 'Eddie's a local?'

Her smile increased. 'He is now, aren't you, sweetheart,' she stated, raising her voice so Eddie could hear them.

'What am I? I can't hear you properly back here.'

She laughed as though Eddie had just said something hilarious. 'Felix here wants to know if you're a local.'

'Ah. *This* is Felix. Sorry. We weren't properly introduced. I'm Eddie. I'm—'

His words were cut off as Harriette's phone buzzed. 'That'll be Tori wanting an update,' she remarked. 'Just as well we're almost there. She is going to be gobsmacked to see you, honey.'

Felix rolled his eyes and looked out of the window. No one seemed to care that Eddie had disrupted the smooth running of the hospital and clinics. It was as though the prodigal son had returned back home and everyone was getting ready for a feast in his honour. The odd thing was that in the three days he'd been in Meeraji Lake, he couldn't remember Eddie's name ever being spoken—not once. Eddie, however, seemed to know exactly who he was.

'How's Chloe been sleeping?' he asked from the back. 'Getting any better?'

'How do you know about Chloe?' Felix glared at Harriette. Had she been telling her 'special someone' all about him? About Chloe?

'Here we are,' Harriette stated as she pulled into the hospital driveway and drove the ambulance back into the garage. No sooner had she stopped the vehicle than Eddie had opened the back doors and loped inside the hospital, leaving Harriette to grab the duffel bag before heading inside. 'Come on. We'll miss Tori's reaction.'

'I'm fine,' Felix muttered, not particularly caring about Tori's reaction to the energetic Eddie. What was so special about him? Felix checked the ambulance was locked up, then caught sight of his reflection in the window, only then realising he was scowling. He wasn't too keen on this Eddie bloke because Eddie had disrupted the calm Felix had only just managed to achieve.

True, there was still a lot of turbulence in his life, mainly thanks to Chloe, but with Harriette's help even that had started to settle down a bit. Now Eddie had come into the mix and the search for calmness would need to start again because no doubt Harriette would want Eddie to stay at the doctors' residence. The entire situation was exactly what Felix didn't need right now, and neither did Chloe. This would create more disruption in her life. Couldn't Harriette see that?

When Felix entered the ED, it was to find Harriette with her arm around Eddie's waist. Eddie looked as though he was tolerating the embrace.

'What a scamp, eh?' Tori remarked when she saw Felix. 'Can you believe what Eddie did in order to surprise Harriette? Crazy.' Tori didn't wait for Felix to answer but instead bid them farewell, heading back to clinic.

'OK,' Eddie said, extricating himself from Harriette's arms. 'I'm gonna go get settled in, then say g'day to some people.' He picked up his duffel and slung it over his shoulder, looking every bit like a handsome superhero, with his blond hair and blue eyes, tanned skin and perfectly straight white teeth.

'Make sure you see Erica. She'll be mad if you don't.'

Eddie grinned and winked at her. 'Yes, Mum,' he said in a teasing tone before walking out of the door. She laughed again and once more Felix found the sound to be like music to his ears. What he didn't like was that Eddie had been the one to make her laugh. Why this should bother him, he really wasn't sure. He only knew that it did and that simply made him mad at himself.

Harriette sighed and sat in the chair, looking very relaxed and at peace. Her eyes were bright, her pink lips held the faint hint of a smile…a smile he wouldn't mind tasting. Felix blinked and immediately looked away from her, one hundred percent confused as to where that thought had come from. Why on earth would he be interested in tasting Harriette Jones's lips? In kissing her? She clearly had that avenue of her life all sorted out thanks, once again, to her special Eddie.

'We will be eating well tonight, my friend,' she remarked, rubbing her hands together with glee.

'Pardon?' He glanced at her and thankfully didn't experience any immediate pangs of jealousy or the need to gather her close and kiss her senseless. Good. He was a grown man and, as such, was more than capable of controlling his libido.

'Dinner tonight. Eddie's going to cook.'

'How do you know?' It also appeared there was no changing the subject from the latest arrival in Meeraji Lake. He opened the next file in the pile and tried to study it, displaying an air of nonchalance as he interacted with Harriette. 'Did he say something?'

'No, but he always cooks the first meal whenever he comes to see me. It's a rule.'

'A rule? Whose rule?'

'Mine.'

Frowning, Felix eased back in the chair and looked at her. 'You make him cook dinner for you whenever you see him?' he clarified, as if trying to make sense of the conversation.

'Yes. I didn't pay for him to go to culinary school for nothing.'

'You paid for—?' Felix held up his hand. 'Wait. What? You paid for your boyfriend to get his qualifications as a chef and in return he has to cook you a meal whenever he comes to—' He stopped again, because Harriette had started laughing again, but this time it was definitely something *he'd* said that was making her crack up.

'What? What did I say?' His words only made her laugh harder. In another moment, she had tears in her eyes and was wiping them. 'What's so funny?' His earlier annoyance and frustration returned and he tossed the pen back onto the desk before sighing with exasperation.

'Oh. Oh, Felix. Thank you. I'm incredibly flattered.'

'Why?' He was totally lost now. Had no clue what she was going on about.

'You think Eddie's...' she stopped, another bout of laughter bubbling through her '...my... my boyfriend?'

Felix frowned, now knowing he'd definitely missed something. She'd kissed Eddie. She'd hugged Eddie. She'd called him sweetheart and honey. How was he *not* to think Eddie was her boyfriend? 'Your...brother? Nephew?'

She laughed again, sniffed and wiped at her eyes. 'No, you absolute ninny. Eddie's my son.' She reached for a tissue and dabbed at her eyes before chuckling again.

'Your *son*! How old are you?'

Harriette's answer was to laugh again, then stand from her chair. 'He even called me "Mum".'

'I just thought he was being ironic.'

Another burst of laughter. 'Well, as we're all quiet here, I think I'll give Tori a hand in the clinic with the immunisations.'

'You're going to tell her, aren't you?' Felix stated, shaking his head with slight embarrassment. 'You don't have to, you know. It was an honest mistake.'

'Yes, but it was a hilarious mistake.' With that, she sauntered out of the ED, still chuckling to herself.

'Her *son*?' he mumbled as he tried to focus on the paperwork before him. How was that possible? Either she was much older than he'd thought or Eddie was much younger than he looked. Or both. It also put the prank at the airfield into better perspective. The son, eager to see his mother, to surprise her, doing a crazy stunt without thinking through or considering the ramifications. It also explained why Harriette had been so happy.

'He was her son.' He shook his head in bemusement. 'It was an honest mistake,' he grumbled as he once again tried to focus his thoughts on the paperwork before him. When he'd finished at the hospital that night, he headed to the doctor's residence, already having received a call from Harriette to check it was all right for her to collect Chloe from day care. As he walked in the door his senses were filled with the most delicious aroma, along with the sound of laughter.

He went into the lounge room and found Eddie lying on the floor on his back, his knees bent, his feet on Chloe's hips and his hands holding her firmly as she stretched out her arms as though she were flying, giving her an aeroplane ride.

'Look at me! I'm flying!'

Harriette sat next to them clapping her hands. Her hair was loose, freed from its messy bun, and when she glanced up at him, the red shoulder-length tendrils curling a little at the end, softening her face and making her look even younger, Felix felt a tightening in his gut. How was it possible that this woman could have a grown-up child? And how was it possible he was no longer in control of his senses? Clearly his self-control required even more work than he'd thought.

'All done?' she checked and he nodded, momentarily unable to speak, he was so captivated by her beauty. 'Doesn't dinner smell delicious? I told you Eddie would cook something brilliant.' Chloe was calling to him, demanding his attention, demanding he comment on her excellent flying skills. Felix obliged, making sure he put the correct amount of enthusiasm into his tone because he'd discovered the hard way that if he didn't, she'd get cross with him and a cross Chloe was not something he had the energy to deal with right now.

'Glass of wine?' Harriette asked as she walked into the kitchen, taking another glass from the cupboard and putting it next to the two wine glasses already on the table.

'Eddie's old enough to drink?'

Her answer was to laugh but not provide him with an answer so he simply had to presume Harriette's son was either over the legal drinking age or she simply didn't care. She poured Felix some wine and handed him the glass, picking up her own and clinking it gently to his. 'Cheers.'

'Cheers,' he returned and they both sipped their wine. 'Mmm. This is delicious. What is it?'

'Burgundy,' Eddie called. 'Perfect to go with the boeuf bourguignon.'

'You've made boeuf bourguignon?' Felix's mouth started salivating at the flavours he knew would come.

'Yes, sir,' Eddie replied.

'I haven't had that for…well, for quite a while.'

'Eddie's been studying in France. Paris, actually, on a scholarship. I'm so proud of my boy.'

Felix sat down at the table, watching as Eddie now crawled around the floor with Chloe, pretending to be lions in the African jungle. 'Does everyone get along with Chloe better than me?' he grumbled.

'It's not like that.' She smiled at him and again he felt as though he'd been kicked in the gut and winded. She was so caring, so positive, so optimistic. 'Just give Chloe a little longer. That's all it's going to take and then she'll be fine.' She grinned then. 'Well, not *fine*, per se. She's almost four, and four-year-olds know absolutely everything about the world. That's what she told me earlier on.'

'She knows everything?'

'That's what she told me when we were walking home from day care. She said, "Harriette, I already know about everything in the world," then she paused and looked quite quizzical before adding, "except juggling. I don't know how to juggle." I couldn't help but crack up laughing. She's quite the comedienne,' she finished.

Felix couldn't help but smile at hearing this exchange. 'Chloe said that?'

'She did. She's very intelligent for her age and her vocabulary is extensive. Quite a smart little cookie.'

'I'm not a cookie,' Chloe called out.

'Nothing wrong with her hearing,' Harriette mumbled with a smile.

'Hey, Chloe,' Eddie said a moment later. 'Do you want to come and help me finish unpacking my bag? There might be a present in there for you.'

'A present? For me?' She clutched her little hands to her chest, her eyes wide in astonishment.

'Yes. Come on. Let's go find it.'

'Yay, yay, yay.Presents!'

'He brought her a gift?' Felix asked.

'Looks that way.'

'Clearly you've told him about me...er...and her...about us...er...being here and—'

'I chat over the Internet with Eddie as much as I can or else we text or call each other so, yes, of course I told him you'd arrived. He was getting worried that I was working myself into an early grave. Naturally, I told him I'd been through worse and being the sole doctor in town was nothing new to me.' She took a sip of her wine before continuing. 'I think if he hadn't come and helped me move here, meeting everyone and seeing I would be well supported, he might never have accepted the scholarship to study in Paris.' Harriette shook her head in bemusement. 'I still can't believe he's here. He's travelled all that way just to see *me*. Now that type of action definitely warms a mother's heart.'

'You're...friends with your son?'

'Of course. It's always been just Eddie and me so there was no other real alternative but to get along.' As she spoke, her expressions and tone filled with pride and happiness as well as pure maternal love for her son, Felix once again found himself staring at her in awe. Parenting was hard. That was a fact he'd always known, especially from the way his own parents had often clashed with him and his brother, but seeing the man Eddie had clearly become, seeing how he clearly adored his mother, how he was accepted by the community and how quickly Chloe had taken to him, was a testament to how well Harriette had raised him. She deserved to be proud of him.

Would he be proud of Chloe one day? Would she want to spend time with him when he was old and grey? Humouring him? Surprising him? He honestly hoped so. It was an odd thing to realise that he *wanted* Chloe to like him, that he wanted her to one day love him. Did he love her? He most certainly cared about her otherwise he wouldn't be here, doing what he was doing.

Felix paused, wanting to ask her a lot of private questions, wanting to know more about her past. Would she find them too invasive? Well, he'd soon find out. He took another sip of his wine, then cleared his throat. 'How old were you when you had Eddie?'

'Sixteen. I got accidentally pregnant on my sixteenth birthday. My boyfriend dumped me the moment I told him about the baby and my parents kicked me out when I refused to get an abortion.'

'Your parents *wanted* you to get an abortion?'

'Yes. They said that having a child so young would ruin my life and that I'd never get into medical school, which was all I'd ever wanted. They called me a disappointment and a few choice other names, then told me to pack my bags and never come home again.'

'While you were pregnant?'

'Yes. Four weeks pregnant. Not even showing but, still, I was a disgrace.'

'What about Eddie's father? He didn't support you in any way?'

'No. He's never wanted anything to do with Eddie. He's married now, with a young family of his own, but still refuses to have anything to do with his oldest son, still declares that Eddie isn't even his.' Harriette shrugged as though she didn't really care but Felix could read between the lines. Eddie's father was a coward, who had taken the easy way out, not only shirking his responsibility towards his son but accusing Harriette of sleeping around. Felix clenched his jaw at the injustice.

'So you were kicked out of home and left to raise a child on your own?' Felix stared at her, completely in awe of the woman before him.

'Yes.'

'And you not only did that but somehow managed to get a medical degree?'

'Yes, I did. The degree took a bit longer than the average medical student but I got there in the end.'

'And now you're almost finished your surgical training?'

'Oral exams at the end of the year and then I'm a bona fide general surgeon. Had to pull a few strings to get my supervisor to sign off on me finishing my registrar training here in Meeraji Lake.'

'And how old is Eddie?'

'Twenty-two.'

'You're thirty-eight? You've raised a child, put yourself through medical school and now surgical registrar training and you're not even forty?'

'What can I say? Some people in the world are clearly over-achievers and I'm one of them.' Harriette took another sip of her wine and he could see he was starting to make her feel a little embarrassed.

Felix stared at her, quite unashamedly, regarding her with appreciation and awe. 'Wow.'

CHAPTER FIVE

'Wow?'

Felix grinned. 'Not a word I often use, Dr Jones, so count yourself fortunate.'

'OK. I will.' Harriette looked at him in confusion, not quite sure how to deal with him in such a mood as this. It wasn't that it was bad seeing him like this; in fact, it was quite the opposite. It was good. Good to see Felix smiling and relaxing a bit and using words he didn't usually use. However, seeing him smile in such a way, seeing the way his eyes seemed to relax from their constant state of stress, seeing the lines soften around his brow, only made him even more appealing and that really was the last thing she needed. Admitting he was a handsome man was one thing, constantly staring and ogling him was another. She shook her head slightly in order to clear her thoughts. 'But what do you mean by...*wow*?'

'It means I've always thought I had a rough life.

My father had undiagnosed post-traumatic stress disorder after serving in the military and my mother did everything she could to hold things together. Then she…er…died and Dad blamed me for her death. I transferred to a different medical school. I needed distance from my father's constant tirades and left David behind—or at least that's how he saw it.'

'What happened?'

'With David?' At Harriette's nod, he hesitated for a moment then shrugged as though keeping silent really wasn't such an issue. 'David was… David was headstrong, right from the start. If there was a kid in the neighbourhood who would come a cropper, then it was David. Fell off his bike, fell off the swings, ran into a tree, got into a fight.' He chuckled. 'Broke his arm, broke his nose, skinned his knees, twisted his ankle. Mum was always taking him to the hospital to be patched up.' Felix spread his arms wide. 'If there was trouble to be found, David found it before anyone else.'

'Sounds as though you were close back then?'

'We were…brothers. We fought, we argued but we'd stick up for each other when it counted most. Until I went to medical school.' He looked up at the ceiling, as though trying to peer back into his past. 'All I could see was an escape from my father's constant berating, constant emotional negative abuse. David saw it as me deserting him. Then when Mum died… David was left to deal with Dad on his own and, from what David told me, Dad was a constant mixture of anger, aggression and antagonism.'

'But you were able to forgive and reconnect, right?'

'To a point. We met up after he married Susan and he sent me a picture of Chloe when she was born. Apart from that it was birthday and Christmas cards.'

Chloe and Eddie had come back into the lounge room, Chloe very eager to show both Felix and Harriette the colouring-in book and pencils Eddie had given her as a gift. 'And I know that I don't draw on the table but only the paper and Eddie's going to colour in with me, aren't you, Eddie? And then we can show you the picture and it's from France!' She flicked open the book and, sure enough, there were a few words here and there in the colouring-in book that were in French. 'And

Eddie's going to teach me what they say. That one—' She pointed to one next to the black outline of a princess. 'That one means "beautiful". *Belle,*' she repeated, glancing across at Eddie as though to ensure she was correct. When he nodded, she said the French word again then raced away to kneel down at the coffee table, settling herself comfortably so she and Eddie could colour in.

'And do you still think you've been dealt a horrible hand?' she asked softly so Chloe couldn't hear. 'Becoming guardian of Chloe?'

Felix sighed thoughtfully and sipped his wine and she could see the shutters starting to come down on his expression. 'I did in the beginning.'

'And now?'

He leaned back in his chair and took another sip of his wine. He wasn't used to speaking so openly about his life, his plans, his past. He kept himself to himself and that was the way it went. If people didn't like it, they could lump it. He was a good surgeon, focused on his job and now he was expected to play happy families? It still didn't sit well with him, especially as Chloe seemed to accept other people far more easily than she'd accepted him.

'I'm just taking it one day at a time. I know more about this parenting caper than I did yesterday.'

She nodded. 'One day at a time. Good concept.'

Felix stood and walked to the kitchen window. He could almost feel Harriette watching him, waiting patiently for him to talk. He didn't want to talk. Didn't want to open up. In the past when he'd allowed himself to be vulnerable, he'd ended up being hurt. He'd loved his mother and she'd died. He'd loved his ex-wife and she'd left him because he'd worked too much and didn't want to have children. Then his last relationship had ended because he'd become guardian to a bereaved three-year-old. Now, though, no matter what he did, for the next fifteen years at the least his first priority would need to be Chloe.

Felix looked at her over his shoulder. 'How did you cope? Young, single mother...how did you cope?'

Harriette shrugged. 'I don't know. I just did.' She thought for a moment more. 'I guess I chose not to let it beat me. I chose to look on the bright side, and that bright side was Eddie. He was my everything. Still is. Without him, everything I do in life has no meaning. I like being in small communities rather than big cities because it allowed me to spend more time with my son. When he's not here—which is still a huge adjustment for me—I focus on getting through the day so I can share it with him over the phone or via email.' She raised her arms in the air. 'Thank God for technology!'

'Are you always this optimistic?'

She chuckled, then shrugged a shoulder. 'I guess so because I couldn't bear to be the alternative.'

'A realist?'

'Nice try. I meant a pessimist. I am a realist—sometimes. If I wasn't, Eddie wouldn't be living on the other side of the world but I know he needs to walk his own path. I guess it all comes down to deciding whether the glass is half full or half empty; whether you're facing struggles or challenges? Perspective. It does make a difference.'

'Chloe's eating and sleeping.' Felix nodded. 'She's healthy and safe.'

'Exactly.'

'Were you always this positive? Even before you became pregnant?'

Harriette thought for a moment. 'I was always determined, especially when my parents kicked me out.'

'Where did you go?'

'First I went to my boyfriend's house.'

'Eddie's father?'

'Yes, but I received the same treatment from him and his parents. I was a disgrace.' She shook her head. 'They called me all sorts of names, accusing me of trying to trap their son, that he wasn't that type of boy, that he had a bright future ahead of him and they weren't going to let me "soil" his reputation by spreading lies, touting him as the father. So I ended up sneaking into my best friend's room and sleeping on her floor, but she didn't want her mother to know I was there because her mother and my mother were good friends.'

'Did you have the entire neighbourhood against you?'

'It was a…tight-knit community.' Harriette laughed without humour. 'My parents were incredibly hypocritical. They cared about what the community thought of them but if I'd had a quiet abortion, if I'd agreed to kill my child—their grandchild—*my Eddie*, then all would be forgiven and I could continue living at home. No one, except the three of us, would ever know what had happened but because I'd told my boyfriend, because I'd told his parents and my best friend, I had brought utter humiliation upon them.'

'You have got to be joking.' Felix's entire body was tense with anger at how she'd been treated. 'No one, especially a young, impressionable girl, deserves to be treated that way, especially when it takes two to tango.' He drew in a breath and forced himself to relax his clenched fists.

Harriette stood and took her empty glass to the bench and poured herself another glass of wine. 'Thank you and thank goodness times have changed.'

Felix walked to her side and placed his hand on her shoulder, looking into her eyes. His touch was warm and for some reason sent a multitude of tingles flooding throughout her body. His brown eyes were such an amazing colour, like a deep rich chocolate with small flecks of gold here and there. Her breathing hitched at the compassion she saw in his gaze. She hardly knew this man but on some level the story of her past had touched him.

'You've done a fantastic job. Not only with Eddie, but following the career you wanted.' His voice was deep, soft and filled with support. He was looking at her as though she should be recommended for sainthood and the thought made her smile.

'I can't believe you put yourself through medical school with no financial help, with no support.'

'I had Eddie.'

'But he was just a child.' A frown pierced Felix's brow.

'Kids are a great support. Eddie was my biggest fan. I was his mummy. His superhero.' Tears pricked her eyes as she spoke, her voice filled with the utmost love for her son. 'Even when things looked as though they couldn't get any worse, when there were days we didn't have enough money to see us through, Eddie would wrap his arms around my neck and tell me I was doing a good job. That I was the best mumma in the world.'

'You're lucky you had him.' Was that a note of envy in Felix's tone? She wasn't quite sure and, even if it was, it disappeared almost instantly. 'He's an amazing young man.'

She grinned and sighed. 'I'm so proud of him.'

Eddie walked into the room and Felix immediately dropped his hands back to his sides. 'You talking about me? How brilliant I am?' Harriette's smile was answer enough. Eddie bent and kissed her cheek. 'Ya did good, Mum, now shift. You're in my way and the dinner will burn if I don't apply my brilliant skills of expertise.'

'Did I mention he also has the gift of hyperbole?' She laughed.

'Uh…where's Chloe?' Felix asked.

'She's in her room,' Eddie said. 'She has the usual three-year-old's attention span—bored after ten minutes. Does she usually have a bath before dinner?'

'Usually, if she doesn't fight it,' Felix grumbled, and was once again treated to the tinkling of Harriette's laughter. He found it difficult to believe she'd been through so much and yet was still, for all intents and purposes, a very happy, well-adjusted person. She wasn't bitter or angry.

She didn't feel as though she'd been dealt a horrible hand and why? Because she loved her son and had that love returned.

Was it really that simple? To love a child and have that child love you back? Was that all he needed to do to gain the sort of inner happiness he'd been searching for his entire life?

Felix looked at Harriette, who swept her hand in front of her. 'Go, Felix. Become her superhero.'

'Run that bath,' Eddie added encouragingly.

'Superhero work begins by running baths?' Felix quirked an eyebrow at them, showing Harriette that beneath that gruff exterior he often portrayed there was clearly a mischievous side to his personality.

'Absolutely,' she returned with a wide grin and, with that, he headed off to get Chloe's bath ready.

Once the little girl was bathed and dressed for bed, Eddie served up dinner. Felix sat next to Chloe and cut up her food. 'It might be a little spicy for her,' Felix added after chewing an exquisite mouthful.

'We'll see,' Harriette remarked as they watched Chloe take the first mouthful.

She grinned and swallowed and declared the food 'yummy'.

'Really?' Felix seemed surprised.

'And Eddie had a cheese sandwich all ready to go in case she didn't like it,' Harriette remarked.

'Cheese sandwich!' Chloe declared and put her spoon down.

'You spoke too soon, Harriette,' Felix remarked and Eddie immediately went and retrieved the cheese sandwich, with the crusts cut off and in little rectangular finger-sized bites. 'A fancy cheese sandwich,' he continued and Eddie just grinned. Then Eddie dipped one end of the cheese sandwich into the boeuf gravy and held it up to Chloe's lips. The child immediately ate it and asked for more.

'It appears to me, Felix,' Harriette said a while later when they'd all finished their meals, 'that your niece prefers French cuisine.'

'Ugh. Trust me to end up with a child who has upmarket tastes.'

Harriette smiled at him, impressed because his tone held the right level of humour, mixed with the right level of truth and—dared she hope?—

a little bit of love towards the gorgeous girl. She had no doubt that Felix loved Chloe but it wasn't a deep, personal love but more one born out of duty. He'd mentioned his father had served in the military and it made her wonder whether that was what 'love' had been like in his household, one of duty and respect rather than one filled with cuddles and laughter.

When Eddie offered to put Chloe to bed—in her own bed—the child willingly agreed but insisted on a horsey ride to take her to her bedroom. Immediately complying, Eddie crouched down and waited for Chloe to seat herself on his back before making clip-clopping noises as he headed towards Chloe's bedroom.

As they stacked the dishwasher Felix couldn't help but voice his amazement. 'Eddie really is quite a natural with Chloe.'

'He's always had a way with people. He just accepts them for who they are and doesn't judge.'

'You, too. You're a lot like that, very personable, very trusting.'

'Ah, but that blind trust can sometimes get you into a lot of deep water.'

'Eddie's father?'

'Exactly. I believed him when he said he loved me. I trusted him when he said that being intimate was the next step in our future relationship, that he wanted to marry me and be with me forever.'

'And yet you still seem able to trust people you've just met?'

'Like you?' When he only shrugged, she continued. 'I have to trust you, at least in a professional capacity. Out here in the middle of nowhere, we're forced into closed quarters. Living here—' she gestured to the house '—working in the clinic, going off on house calls, which out here last for two or three days because the properties are spread out. We need to trust each other, to be open and honest with each other, rely solely on the other person—especially in an emergency. We're not in a large teaching hospital any more, where there are countless other staff members and a plethora of equipment. It's just you and me and our wits.'

'And our training.'

'That, too.' She smiled. 'What I'm trying to say is, the sooner we figure each other out, the sooner we form an understanding of how each other ticks. That's what small-town medicine is all about—getting to know the staff on a personal level, getting to know your patients on a personal level and thereby being able to provide personalised treatment. When someone gets a cold in this town *everyone* gets a cold. Everyone gets sick together, or it comes in waves, and to deal with that we need to be a *part* of the community rather than standing back from the outside looking in.'

'But in standing back, we may be protected from becoming sick ourselves and therefore will be more able to heal the community from the outside.'

'Fair point but that's just not an option. Your patients won't trust you, they won't tell you what's wrong in the first place and then signs and symptoms risk going untreated and causing more of an epidemic that then spreads throughout the wider districts, infecting more people.'

Felix sighed with exasperation and sat back down on the chair, elbows on the table, head in his hands. 'What have I done, coming here?' The question was rhetorical and Harriette stayed quiet but went and sat down next to him. 'I'm not the sort of bloke who enjoys…closeness of community. I've never had it before. Not in my family growing up and not in my working life. I guess I don't need "closeness" as much as others.'

'Everyone needs to be close to someone, Felix.'

He lifted his head and stared across at her. 'Like you and Eddie?'

'Yes. You can have that closeness with Chloe.'

'But she's only three.'

'Almost four,' Harriette added. 'And yes, you can have that closeness with her. Just because she's a child, it doesn't mean she doesn't have the same feelings. She may not comprehend them in the way you and I do, but she has them and she needs you to help her and the only way you can help her is to *become* an integrated part of her life. If you let her in, if you let her break through that heart of yours, which you've clearly had locked up for quite some time now, then your life will change in all the positive ways you've probably never even imagined.'

Felix stared at her for a moment, then shook his head in stunned bemusement. 'How is it you seem to know me so well?'

'I know your type. Eddie's father was a lot like you.'

'I don't think that's a compliment, given he left you in the lurch.'

'And you wouldn't have?'

'If I had accidentally impregnated my girl-friend, I would not have left her to raise *my* child on her own.' His words were vehement and di-rect and she could see that he meant every sin-gle word. 'There are too many injustices in the world. It's important we fix the ones that are within our control.'

'Would you have offered to pay for an abor-tion?'

'No.' His answer was instant.

'So in your opinion I did the right thing?' She couldn't help the hint of her past inexperienced sixteen-year-old self tingeing her words.

'Of course and meeting Eddie only proves you did the right thing.'

'I think your brother did the right thing by ap-pointing you as Chloe's guardian. Whatever your differences, he knew you'd be able to cope with the situation. That's a compliment.'

Felix leaned back in his chair and laced his

fingers behind his head, stretching his shoulder muscles. Harriette tried not to stare, tried to remember why there were sitting here chatting, that she was trying to help him put his situation into perspective. Instead, she seemed to be memorising the way his shirt was pulled taut across his well-defined biceps and how the buttons looked as though they were ready to burst as his chest expanded beneath the fabric. She closed her eyes for a split second, determined to focus and get her over-active hormones under control.

'Once or twice a year,' Felix began and Harriette looked at him again. Thankfully, he'd stopped stretching and was rubbing his temples with his fingers. 'David would get himself into some sort of trouble and I'd either get a call while I was away at medical school, from my father telling me to "handle it" or from the police. The area where David and my father still lived was where I went to high school and two of the police officers at the local station were in my year so nine times out of ten they'd call me first, rather than having to deal with my father.'

Harriette raised her eyebrows in surprise. 'The police didn't like your father?'

'Post-traumatic stress disorder, especially when triggered through serving in a war zone, doesn't bring out the best in people who suffer from it.' He clasped his hands in front of him and placed them on the table. 'My father's moods were erratic. One minute you'd be having a normal conversation with him and the next, he'd be yelling at you to get down under the table, to protect yourself. He'd accuse you of taking his gun, of being in collusion with the enemy.' Felix looked down at his hands and only then realised just how tightly he was clenching his fingers. He forced himself to relax, to take a deep and calming breath.

'David's antics were often more than enough to set Dad off. Sometimes, he'd think David or I were the enemy and he'd hit us. Then, when he snapped out of it, he would apologise profusely, often in tears, begging us to forgive him and not report him.'

'You poor boys.' Harriette's heart went out to the younger Felix, feeling sad for what he'd endured.

'I think Mum hid it from us for quite a while, managed it by getting him onto anti-depressants, which seemed to help with the symptoms, but after her…death, he just snapped. He was never the same, never fully comprehensive of what the life around him was all about.' Felix spoke softly, looking past Harriette as though he was looking back in time. 'Life could have been so different for us all. We wouldn't have been so estranged. It would have made Mum sad to know that that's how things ended up. David and I not talking. Dad turning his back on both of us, declaring us "dead to him", not wanting to talk to us, to have anything to do with us.' His voice was soft, reflective and filled with regret. He was so lost in his thoughts that he was surprised when Harriette put her hand over his, offering support. When he returned his gaze to meet hers, he was even more astonished to find she had tears in her eyes.

'Wow.' The word was soft and she sniffed, offering him a wobbly smile.

'Wow?' He mimicked her earlier response.

'And I thought I'd had a hard life.'

Felix couldn't help but smile. 'I guess we…everyone…has their own crosses to bear.'

'It's how we deal with them, how we allow them to shape us as a person, that matters most.'

She rubbed her fingers slowly on top of his in a gesture of support and understanding. She'd been through her own personal hell and she'd conquered it. And yet, he was still surprised at how one simple touch from her was really starting to make him feel better about his past. That sort of thing had never happened to him before. Then again, he'd rarely spoken to anyone about his family. Even with his ex-wife and definitely not with his last girlfriend. So what was it about Harriette that was making him open up, making him tell her things he'd never have thought of telling her?

Was it because she was such a calm and confident woman who, as he'd witnessed over the past few days, was very empathetic towards her patients, the staff and basically everyone she met? Or was it because she had the ability to make him feel as though he was the most important person in the world right now, that all her attention was focused solely on him, that she was *listening* to him.

'Where is he now?' Her soft words brought his thoughts back to what they'd been discussing, even though he was still highly aware of her smooth, soft hand resting on top of his.

'My father?' At her nod, he continued. 'In a nursing home in Darwin. It's one for ex-service-men and especially those suffering from PTSD and other associated disorders. He has demen-tia now and wouldn't have a clue who I was. I receive regular emailed updates from his physi-cian and the last one stated that the old man was slowly failing.'

'Oh, Felix. Darwin isn't that far from here. You could go and visit him. Dale could fly you there as soon as you like.'

Felix withdrew his hand from her touch and stood. 'Why would I want to see him? He hasn't spoken to me in years. He told me I was useless, hopeless and a disgrace. He blamed me for my mum's death, he accused me of—' He stopped and shook his head. 'No. I don't want to see him.'

As though he couldn't stay still, Felix started to pace back and forth in front of her. 'Do you see your parents? Especially after the way they treated you? Treated Eddie?' He clearly wanted the conversation turned away from himself and the only way he could do this was to attack her.

Thankfully, Harriette recognised this behaviour and answered the question calmly, rather than allowing him to rile her as had clearly been his intention. She knew what emotional pain was like and she knew it could make you do and say things you often wished unsaid.

'Yes. I tried many times over the years and they refused any contact but then, when Eddie was twelve, he ended up in hospital with influenza A. It was the darkest time of my life. Nothing… no hurt, no pain—*nothing*—could compare with the thought of losing my boy. We had to go to Melbourne city so Eddie could receive treatment. I called my parents. I begged them to come to the hospital and…eventually they did. It wasn't a tear-filled reunion and we still don't talk regularly but at least I know I can contact them if I need to and vice versa.'

'You forgave them? After the way they treated you? Treated Eddie?'

She shrugged. 'You just do because otherwise it eats at you. You end up with regrets and if you leave it too late, those regrets can affect your life.'

He knew what she meant. He had so many regrets but they were to do with his mother, not his father. 'Mother.' He whispered the word, barely audible but somehow Harriette heard.

'You have regrets about your mother?' she asked softly.

Felix swallowed and clenched his jaw as though he was desperately trying to control his over-wrought emotions. 'Yes.' He choked on the word and lowered his head to look at the ground, his hands curled tight into fists at his sides.

'Everything changed when she died?' Harriette offered when he didn't say anything more.

'Yes.'

'You loved her.' It was a firm statement.

He raised his head and met her gaze. She could see the anguish in his eyes, could see the sorrow and regret in his face. 'Yes.'

If all Felix was capable of was monosyllabic answers then she would provide him with the easiest way to get through this difficult conversation because now that he'd unlocked the doors he'd obviously kept closed for quite a few decades, she didn't want him to slam them shut again, especially not when his father was dying.

'Do you think your mother would want you to go see him? Even if he doesn't know who you are?'

It took a while for him to answer. 'Yes.' He cleared his throat. He looked so much like a little lost boy that her maternal instincts kicked in and she instantly stood and walked to his side. He remained where he was, body taut, hands clenched, jaw tight. He was still looking at her, still holding her gaze, still trying to shut her out but clearly unable to do so. Harriette was honoured. She placed her hands onto his shoulders.

'Would you like me to go with you?' She held her breath as she waited for him to answer. It was a turning point in his life. Would he choose to heal his past or would he live with regret for ever? He clearly regretted the rift between his brother David and himself. Would he miss the same opportunity with his father? She continued to hold his gaze, not wavering but trying to support him, with whatever decision he made. She silently prayed it was the right one. That he would go.

'Yes.'

The instant he said the word, Harriette breathed out and then, as though it was the most natural thing in the world, she slipped her arms under his and allowed him to draw her close into a hug. It wasn't a hug filled with sensual over-tones, although she wasn't unaware of just how perfectly his body was sculpted. Instead, it was a hug between friends—friends who were be-coming closer with every passing moment. By agreeing that he wanted her to go with him on this venture, he was showing her just how much he was putting his trust in her.

'I won't let you down,' she whispered against his chest and closed her eyes, his firm, solid arms still enfolded around her.

'Thank you.'

CHAPTER SIX

FOR A LONG moment Felix stood there with his arms around Harriette, unable to believe that this woman had not only managed to get him to open up about his family, and more particularly his father, and was now hugging him close, offering her support.

He wasn't used to people supporting him, being on his side. In fact, every woman he'd ever dared to care about had rejected him in one way or another. Harriette might be saying she'd support him now but she'd leave him in the end. Although she'd offered to come and see his father with him, she would forget about it, or she'd find an excuse.

He stopped the thought before it began and adjusted his arms around Harriette, trying to loosen his hold a little as he became more aware of just how perfectly she fitted into his arms. He tried not to breathe in her alluring scent, tried to remember that she was only hugging him because she'd been emotionally moved by what he'd told her. A woman like her, a woman who appeared genuine and naturally caring, couldn't possibly be interested in a career-hungry surgeon who didn't know the first thing about raising a child.

Felix shifted back a little, knowing he needed to let her go before he started to memorise the contours of her body pressed against his own. Harriette. Sweet Harriette. During the past few days she'd helped him more than she'd realised. Gratitude was one thing but starting to become more aware of her as a woman was a completely different thing altogether.

Harriette lifted her head and looked up at him, concern still reflected in her gaze. 'We'll get through this together. You're not alone.'

He nodded and edged back from her, trying not to be delighted when she took her time sliding her hands from his waist. Was she trying to linger? Could she feel that same awareness buzzing between them?

'We should probably go and say goodnight to Chloe.'

'Uh…' He cleared his throat. 'Yes. Good.'

Harriette walked ahead of him and he followed,

trying not to watch the way her hips swayed gently from side to side, trying not to feel bereft because she wasn't in his arms any more. They were colleagues. Yes, he was a man and yes, she was an incredibly attractive woman, but if this whole situation was going to work he needed to get himself under better control. Focusing on Chloe would definitely help and, when they entered her room, they found the little girl all snuggled up in bed, almost asleep. She was still awake enough to know they were there. Eddie finished reading the last page of the book using a boring monotone voice, then grinned at his mother before standing and heading out.

Felix watched in the dim light of the room as Harriette knelt down beside Chloe's bed and tenderly brushed some hair from the little girl's forehead before placing a gentle kiss there. She whispered sweet and soothing words to the child, just as a mother would. Just as his mother had when he'd been little. He could remember her coming into the room he'd shared with David. He'd been almost eight years old and had been begging for his own room. His mother had told him that when they moved to the next military posting, onto the military base, he would be able to have his own room. He'd told her that when that happened, he wouldn't need her to come in and say goodnight to him like this, to brush her hand on his forehead and place a kiss there. He would be too old for that ritual and she need not bother. His mother's answer had been to chuckle softly and kiss his forehead. 'I will always come and kiss you goodnight,' she'd told him. 'You're my wonderful son, no matter how old you are.'

Felix tried to swallow over the dryness of his throat before forcing himself to block out his emotions surrounding his mother. She'd lied to him, she'd let him down and she'd left him and David alone in the world to fend for themselves.

'Did you want to give her a little kiss? She's practically asleep right now.'

Felix blinked, bringing his thoughts back to the present at Harriette's soft question. He looked at her. 'Pardon?'

She smiled and beckoned for him to kneel down next to her. He hesitated for a moment, then did as Harriette had suggested. As he bent down his knee cracked and Harriette immediately grinned. 'Getting old,' he mumbled.

'Aren't we all?' she whispered back.

'Not you.' The words were instant. Harriette continued to stroke Chloe's hair and a moment or two later, the child's breathing evened out into a natural rhythm. 'You don't look old enough to have a twenty-two-year-old son.' He gestured to the sleeping Chloe. 'A child of this age—yes, but the mother of a grown man? Most definitely no.'

Harriette looked at him for a moment, a look of surprise and...embarrassment? Had he embarrassed her?

'Sorry. It wasn't my intention to embarrass—'

'You didn't,' she responded quickly, perhaps too quickly. As they both knelt beside Chloe's bed, side by side, leg near leg, arm near arm, Felix realised far too late just how close they were to each other. He breathed in her scent, allowing it to wind its way around him, to become absorbed by his senses. 'I...er...it was very nice of you to say that. You know, that I look young.'

He was learning not to be astounded or even surprised at her openness. Harriette would talk about any subject with him in an honest way and that promoted a faith in her, the beginnings of trust. Of course, on a professional level, there was already a certain level of trust forming between them, but this was a deep, personal kind of trust and he wasn't sure when he'd last felt that way about anyone.

'Surely you know how beautiful you are, Harriette.' His soft words were a statement and for a long moment they stared into each other's eyes. It was as though time stood still, as though it were only the two of them. That seemed to be happening to him…to them…a lot lately. Would it continue? As he settled into life in Meeraji Lake, would this sensation, these feelings, the attraction he felt towards her continue to grow? Did he want that?

'Well…uh…I guess that doesn't…um…really matter.' Her stuttered words weren't the reaction he was expecting. In fact, he wasn't sure exactly what reaction he'd been expecting but he didn't expect her to stand and walk away. He *had* embarrassed her, or at the least he'd made her feel uncomfortable. Felix turned and watched Chloe sleeping, shaking his head slowly from side to side.

'Women,' he murmured softly but in a way that held such confusion and bewilderment. 'I doubt

I'll ever understand you.' He reached and brushed Chloe's hair from her forehead, mimicking Harriette's actions. He hadn't really done this before, watched Chloe sleep. Usually, as soon as she was asleep, he'd collapse with exhaustion.

As he looked at her, gently touched her smooth, soft forehead, he was filled with a sense of… love. He knew he loved Chloe, in the sense that she was his niece and it was his duty to love her, but to be so completely stirred by the emotion, to look at this angelic little person—the same little person who he'd hardly class as angelic when she was awake and causing complete havoc in his life—and have his heart fill with love for her… He paused, then leaned forward and pressed a kiss to her forehead.

The instant his lips touched her baby-soft skin a warmth flooded through him and seemed to spread throughout his entire body. A warmth of affection, a warmth of protection, a warmth of devotion. He eased back and stared at the child in complete bewilderment. Even though she'd caused him deep consternation, deep confusion and deep contemplation, even though she'd screamed so loud he'd thought his ear drums would burst, even though she'd turned his life inside out and upside down... Felix loved her. Not because he *had* to love her but because he *wanted* to love her.

He stood and once again stared at the sleeping angel. 'Huh!' Then he turned and stopped short when he saw Harriette leaning against the door jamb. 'I thought you'd gone.'

'It's amazing, isn't it?' she stated quietly.

'What?'

'The moment you're completely overcome with parental love for your child.'

Felix shoved his hands into his pockets, unsure he was ready to discuss the emotions he'd just experienced. They were still too raw and personal for him to talk about, especially when he wasn't even sure he understood them.

'She's my niece,' he murmured as he walked past Harriette, feeling a different sensation— one of close awareness—as he made sure their bodies didn't accidentally brush each other as he headed into the living room.

'She's your *daughter*,' Harriette corrected. Eddie wasn't anywhere to be found so she assumed he'd gone to his own bedroom.

'No, she's not. She's David's daughter. In my mind, she will always be David's daughter and I'll always be Uncle Felix.'

'In *your* mind, yes, but in her mind, she will come to see you as her father.'

'Hmm.' He hadn't thought about it that way before. He sat down in the chair and gave it some serious consideration. 'She'll always know her true parentage. Even if she forgets David and Susan, I'll remind her, I'll show her photos of them, tell her anecdotes about them.'

'Of course.'

'But she'll see me as her father. She'll be my daughter.'

Harriette sat down in the chair opposite and kept quiet, delighted at watching the dawning realisation cross his face.

'Chloe is legally my child, my *daughter*.' He paused and allowed that previous sensation of love, the love he felt towards the girl, wash over him once more. 'I'm not just her guardian, I'm her…*father*!' His mind seemed to race, to connect dots that he'd never noticed before. 'I'd never wanted children before because of…well, because of many reasons but now that it's finally sinking in...' He looked at Harriette. 'I want to be a good father.'

'And you will.'

'How can you know that?'

'Because we're having this conversation. There will be a lot of questioning, a lot of arguments, a lot of love and, believe me, it's all well worth it.'

'But *how* do I do it? How do I become a good dad?'

Harriette leaned back in the chair and grinned. 'Get to know Chloe.'

He waited for more advice but it never came. 'That's it? The wise and sage advice you're offering is "get to know Chloe"?'

'Yep, but *really* get to know her.'

'How?' He leaned forward in his chair and spread his arms wide, his face earnest, his words filled with incredulity. 'How do I do that? No one will tell me how. I've read about a hundred parenting books and articles online but none of them are written out like hospital protocols. None of them say, "Do this and then do that." So what am I supposed to do, Harriette? Tell me, please. How do I get to know her?'

Harriette was laughing at him but not in a mean

way, more in a way that told him she was as surprised by his outburst as he was. 'OK. OK. I'll help you. I'll tell you the secret to parenting.'

'There's a secret?'

'Well, there's a few and the first one you need to know is—be interested in what they're interested in.'

'Be interested.' He nodded. 'What else?'

She thought for a moment. 'It doesn't get better, it just gets different.'

'More riddles? What is that supposed to mean?'

'It means that whatever phase your child is going through, it's never going to get better. You can't wait for things to get better, to settle down, because they don't. Just when you think you have a handle on things, when you think you've figured them out, they enter the next phase and—'

'It gets different.' He nodded. 'Anything else?'

Harriette sighed and frowned in thought. 'It's a long time since I've had to do any of these things.'

'So there does come a time when you're done? When the parenting is over?'

'No. When you're a parent, you're a parent for life—if that's what you choose. Eddie is my best friend. I love being with him and I hate it when he goes because I worry about him. That part never goes away.'

'The worry never goes away. Got it.' Felix looked around. 'I should be writing these down.'

'You're a smart man. You'll remember them.'

'But tell me *how...how* do I get interested in what she likes?'

Harriette eased back into the chair and thought for a moment. 'Ask what her favourite book is.'

'Favourite book. Got it. What else?'

'Read stories to her. Ask her which toy is her favourite. What's her favourite colour?'

'She has a favourite colour?'

'Of course she does.'

'What is it? Do you know?'

'You know as well, you just haven't tuned your brain into realising it.'

'You're talking in riddles again.' He leaned back and crossed his arms in an action that immediately reminded her of Chloe.

'What colour is the backpack she takes to day care?'

'Purple.'

'What colour are the shoes she likes to wear the most?'

He thought on this one for a moment. Chloe had a favourite pair of shoes? He pictured the ones she'd been wearing today…and then realised she'd worn them yesterday and the day before and, for that matter, she usually got upset if he tried to make her wear different shoes that were more suitable to the weather. 'Purple.'

'So…her favourite colour is?'

'Purple.' He nodded slowly, as though he was finally starting to see what Harriette was saying. 'Was that why she got angry with me yesterday morning? Because I told her to wear runners to day care rather than her sparkly purple shoes?'

'Yes.'

'Well, why didn't she just say they were her favourite?'

'Because she's three years old.' Harriette laughed.

'Am I supposed to let her get away with doing whatever she wants?'

'She'll *want* to listen to you if you give her good reasons to listen.'

'There you go again. Talking in riddles.'

Harriette shook her head in bemusement. 'You can't cram for a parenting exam. You just learn things over time.'

'I wish it was an exam. It would certainly be easier.'

'To start with, why don't you arrange a play-date with her? That way, you're showing Chloe that you're interested in what she's interested in.'

'But what if I'm actually not interested in the same things as her?'

'Then you learn to be.' Harriette's words were earnest, her gaze direct. 'This is too important, Felix. Your relationship with Chloe is more important than your work, than being published. Patients will come and go. Jobs will come and go. Publications will come and go. Chloe is in your life *forever*. She's a constant in your life, just as you're a constant in hers. So start by spending time together. Just the two of you, or invite some of her day-care friends along if you must, but *you* have to be a part of the event.'

'Event? Like what?'

Harriette thought for a moment. 'Uh…what about a…tea party? Sit down and pretend to have a tea party with her.'

'Pretend? As in make-believe?'

'Yes. Use that rusty imagination of yours. It could do with a good oiling.'

'A tea party?'

'Yes.'

'A pretend tea party.' He mulled over the idea.

'Pretend ones are easier to organise and she'll be less fussy about the food,' Harriette pointed out.

'Good point. She won't get cross with me for cutting her cheese sandwich into squares instead of rectangles if it's imaginary.' Felix rubbed his chin with his thumb and forefinger. 'A tea party, eh?'

'Looks as though you're already getting ideas.'

'Will you come?'

She looked at him with excited surprise. 'Do you want me to?'

'Yes. You and Eddie, Chloe and myself.That way, as it'll be my first time hosting an imaginary tea party, you'll be able to tell me if I'm doing anything wrong.'

Harriette laughed. 'I think Chloe will be the one to tell you if you're doing it wrong. She's very forthright in her opinions.'

'I've noticed.' He closed his eyes for a moment and shook his head.

'That's a good thing, Felix. Just think. When she's older, when guys are interested in her, she's not going to be a pushover. She's going to know exactly what she wants, and she's going to go for it but only if she knows you've got her back.'

'Don't even mention guys. Just the thought of her, all grown up with some pimply, hormonal teenager drooling all over her—' He clenched his hands and shook his head, a protective look in his eyes. Harriette couldn't have been prouder.

'The point is, if she has your support, she'll realise she can do anything in life.'

'And it all starts with a tea party?'

'And it all starts with a tea party,' she confirmed with a bright and happy smile, delighted she'd been able to get Felix not only to open up to her, something she had a feeling he rarely did, but to view his guardianship of Chloe in a different light. He had been blessed with the opportunity to be a parent, to be a father to a grieving, hurting child, and as she watched him declare he was going to go and watch his *daughter*, not his niece, sleep, Harriette was positive she'd seen the imaginary swish of a superhero cape fluttering out from behind him.

CHAPTER SEVEN

IT WAS TWO days later when Harriette received her invitation to join Miss Chloe Jane McLaren and Dr Felix McLaren for a tea party, to be held at half past four in the afternoon, at the doctors' residence. She rushed through her paperwork after clinic and managed to arrive only two minutes late.

'She's here! She's here!' Chloe's excited words filled the house as Harriette stepped inside. Eddie, Chloe and Felix were already in the lounge room where a picnic rug had been spread out on the carpet and a lovely new purple tea set with little white flowers on it, had been set up for four people. Felix stood behind one of the high wing-back chairs, grinning widely at Chloe's over-excitement.

'Look. Look.' Chloe pointed at the tea set as she ran around the edge of the rug with hyperactive delight. 'Uncle Felix bought it for me. For *me* because he said I've been a good girl and it has little flowers on it. Look, Harriette.'

'That's so pretty.'

'And we're having a tea party!' Chloe jumped up and down and clapped her hands, completely and utterly delighted with this turn of events. 'I helped Uncle Felix set it all up and we did it together.'

Harriette glanced at Felix and nodded in approval. 'Very impressive.'

'But the food isn't real but then we can use our 'maginations and have purple tea and orange cupcakes,' the little girl continued, taking Harriette's hand and leading her to a place setting. 'You sit here.'

'All right.'

'And, Eddie, you sit over here.' Chloe led Eddie to his spot, clearly eager to get this tea party underway. 'And, Uncle Felix, you sit over here.' She took Felix's hand and he seemed surprised at Chloe's voluntary act of treating him like the others. 'And I'll sit here because then I'm closest to the teapot and the 'magination food so I can give it all to you.'

'That sounds perfectly lovely,' Harriette said

and then held out her cup to Chloe. 'May I please have a cup of…blue tea?'

Chloe giggled but lifted the pot and poured a cup of imaginary blue tea for her first guest. As the party continued they all pretended to eat the vibrantly coloured food and Eddie made sure Chloe drank her imaginary tea with her little finger in the air.

At some point, Chloe even went into her bedroom and came out with two or three soft toys, declaring that Eddie, Harriette and Uncle Felix had had enough and now needed to go into the kitchen because she had other guests coming for her next tea party. The three-year-old amused herself, playing with her toys and the tea set while the adults dutifully went to the kitchen.

'I'll get the non-imaginary dinner started,' Eddie remarked.

'You don't have to cook for us,' Felix stated. 'I'm happy to do dinner this evening.'

'It's fine. I like cooking for my mum and her friends. Makes me feel as though I'm giving her something back.'

'You know you don't—' Harriette began, reiterating what Felix was saying, but her son silenced her.

'Shh.' He held a finger to his lips and glared at her. 'Enough, Mum.'

'Yes, son,' she remarked with a twinkling smile. Felix watched the exchange between the two of them, astonished at how close they really were. Even before his mother had passed away, he'd never been that close to her. Never in his life would he have 'shushed' his mother, but neither would he have laughed with her or put his arm around her shoulders or given her a kiss on the cheek. It wasn't that she hadn't loved her boys, it was simply that she hadn't been the demonstrative type. Her way of showing them love had been to cook meals, to clean their clothes, and to help proofread their homework. Still, she would come in at night, brush his hair from his forehead and kiss him. She did it with himself and David and only when their father wasn't around.

Felix could recall his father berating his mother, telling her she would make the boys soft, that she would turn them into sissies if she kept cuddling and kissing them all the time. Boys needed to be tough, needed not to cry, needed to shoulder responsibility from a young age or they would never grow up to be men, they would grow up to be sissy men. Felix closed his eyes for a moment, wanting to remove his father's dictatorial and overbearing voice from his mind.

Ever since he'd mentioned that his father was in Darwin, Harriette had been trying to figure out a way for them to go and see him and every time she'd brought the topic up, he'd done his best to shut her down. He regretted telling her about his past and especially about his father. He didn't want to see his father, didn't want anything to do with him. Couldn't she see that? The man was a cold, hard-hearted emotionally abusive—and sometimes physically abusive—soldier with dementia. The old man might not know who Felix was but Felix surely knew who his father was and the more Harriette talked about it, the more he started to retreat, to withdraw from the subject and from her, to put some distance between himself and his new colleague. He'd always been a loner and, although he could acquiesce and make room for Chloe in his life, he wasn't about to make room for anyone else.

Was that the reason why he'd had difficulty

being demonstrative himself? Because he'd been raised by a cold man and a woman who only felt able to show him some affection when his father was nowhere around? Clearly that wasn't the way Eddie had been raised and with what he'd already learned about Harriette, he knew she'd shown him all the affection she could. She'd shared that affectionate heart of hers with the people of this community, with her patients, with him and with Chloe. It was an affection that promoted easy acceptance, that seemed to make insurmountable problems very easy to conquer.

As he half listened to the easy banter between Harriette and her son he realised that, from what she'd said, her own home life hadn't been that loving. Had her parents cuddled her in public? Kissed her in public? Told everyone how proud they were of their daughter, telling them without agenda or self-importance? He guessed not, because if they had truly loved and cared for Harriette they would never have kicked her out of home in the first place and yet here she was, enjoying that loving, caring relationship quite openly with her son.

He remembered how, when she'd first seen

Eddie come down the aeroplane stairs, her eyes had twinkled, her mouth had curved into the biggest smile and her arms had opened wide in order to envelop her most beloved son. He'd never seen a mother behave like that towards her adult child and he'd never seen an adult child behave that way towards his mother. Eddie was more than happy to be seen with her, to spend time with her, to laugh and chat with her friends—whether they be old or young. They accepted each other for who they were, as individuals and as part of a family.

It gave him hope that perhaps one day he and Chloe might have a relationship like Harriette and Eddie. Today he'd been heartened by the way she'd accepted his surprise of having a tea party, of the special tea set he'd ordered online a few days ago and that had been delivered via plane on the daily mail run.

'Where ever did you find that tea set?' Harriette asked him, interrupting his solitary reverie. 'It's absolutely perfect.'

'On the Internet.' Felix shrugged as though the entire thing were no big deal and Harriette couldn't help but laugh and shake her head. Her twinkling eyes said she knew he was being non-chalant, that she knew he would have spent far too much time on the task, determined to get it right.

'Then, I must say, excellent work, Dr McLaren. Perfect choice of colours and pattern in the china.'

'Purple,' he interjected.

'And perfect size. Easy for little fingers to pick up and use.'

Harriette was sitting at the table and Felix joined her, sitting on her right and trying desperately not to knock her knee as he shifted in his chair. Ever since the other night when he'd held her in his arms, he'd become hypersensitive about how close they were, of whether their fingers had touched, whether their knees had knocked together beneath the table. And every time they did accidentally touch, a shot of desire would ripple through him.

It was ridiculous, of course. Harriette was his colleague and the fact that they lived in such close proximity and worked in such close proximity and…ate meals in such close—

'Are you all right, Felix?' Harriette asked, stalling his thoughts. Her head was slightly tipped to the side and she was looking at him with a hint of concern.

'I'm fine. Why?'

'Well...' She cleared her throat and lowered her voice to just above a whisper. 'You're...uh... staring at me.'

'Oh? Was I? Sorry.' He shifted back in his chair, trying to put distance between them. Chloe was in the lounge room still chattering away to her toys and feeding them imaginary food while Eddie was whistling as he worked, chopping vegetables. There were two other people with them and yet Felix felt as though it were just himself and Harriette...close...together...intimate. What was it about this woman that was making him so aware of her? He'd never had this problem before. He'd always been able to control his libido, to control his emotions, but with Harriette... He shook his head.

'What is it?' she asked again, her concern deepening.

'I don't talk about my life.' The words were almost ripped from his vocal box and he surprised himself at the low determination accompanying them.

'So I gathered.'

'What's that supposed to mean?'

Her instant smile disarmed him once more. 'It means that every time I've mentioned your father in the past few days, you've shut me down. Clearly you regret telling me anything and I respect that.'

'You do?'

'That doesn't mean I'm going to stop in my preparations for us to get to Darwin to see him.'

'But—'

'Berate me. Hate me. Never speak to me again.' She shrugged one beautiful shoulder, the cotton strap of her top falling off, exposing the perfect skin beneath. His gaze honed in on the area where her shoulder and neck met and the tingling in his lips, the need and the desire to taste that one spot, roared through him like a heat he'd never felt before. 'You need to see your father before he dies.'

She was speaking words but the reverberating sound of blood pumping furiously around his body was inhibiting him from processing what she was saying. Good heavens. Didn't the woman have any idea just how desirable she was? Why hadn't she married? Why had she remained alone all these years? Why hadn't any man realised how wonderful, caring and giving she was and asked her to marry him? Perhaps some had? Perhaps she'd said no. Perhaps she'd said yes. In fact, he really had no idea whether or not—

'Uncle Felix!'

Chloe's insistent and impatient tone broke through his thoughts and he'd never been more thankful for the interruption. Thinking about Harriette in such a fashion was something he'd been trying to keep at bay. 'Yes?' He turned to face his niece, who had clearly been calling his name a few times.

'I need your help,' she demanded.

'Manners?' Harriette interjected.

'I need your help, *please*, Uncle Felix.' Chloe's instant amendment, not having a tantrum about being reminded to use her manners, showed him just how far the little girl had come in such a short time.

Felix stood and walked over to Chloe, giving her his attention. One of her toys wasn't able to sit up properly and kept falling into his imaginary food.

'I've already had to clean Captain Gumleaf twice and I'm getting tired of it,' the little girl told him and Felix couldn't help but smile.

'I think a cushion will do the trick.' And he took a cushion off the chair and placed it behind the toy, forcing the stuffed koala to sit up properly and behave himself. The toy had been a present from Eddie, an Australian koala to welcome Chloe to her new country. She loved the toy but clearly had expected better manners from him at her tea party.

Felix decided to stay with Chloe, sitting down on the carpet just behind her toys. It was far safer to be here than to go back to sitting at the table with Harriette. He hadn't responded to her declaration that she was going to force him to see his father. Deep down inside he knew she was right. He also knew if he told her to stop, that he was serious about not seeing his father, she would indeed stop. He didn't want to see his father. He didn't want to face his past, but if he didn't would he end up being as distant and as unfeeling with Chloe as his father had been with him?

Chloe. He sighed with resignation as he watched her. No matter what plans he might have had for his life, no matter what sort of father he would make, it didn't change the fact that this little girl was depending on him and he needed to do his best not to make a mess of things. And that included keeping his libido under control.

He glanced over at Harriette, who was now at the kitchen bench helping Eddie with the dinner preparations. The two of them were chatting softly and occasionally laughing. Felix closed his eyes, allowing the tinkling sound of her sweet laughter to wash over him. He wasn't used to connecting with women, not in such an emotional way as he seemed to be doing with Harriette. He was used to dating, to making sure the rules were clear—that his career came first.

That wasn't the case anymore. Chloe came first and that meant anything he felt for Harriette was irrelevant. If, for the sake of argument, the situation between himself and Harriette progressed, they started dating, started to become serious about their relationship, what would it mean for Chloe? He knew Chloe loved Harriette, even more than she might love him, but he was Chloe's guardian, not Harriette. Besides, he didn't even know if Harriette wanted to be in a relationship where a child was involved. Did she want to have more children or, now that Eddie was a grown man, was she done? There was still so much he didn't know about her, so much he wanted to ask but had no idea how to go about it, given he wasn't used to prying in other people's lives.

It wasn't as though they hadn't talked. They had, because with Eddie here for the past few days, once Chloe had been in bed, the three of them had sat up chatting.

Eddie told stories of his travels, of backpacking through Europe and how he was now learning German as well as French.

'Would you like to go to Germany to cook as well?' Felix had asked one evening.

Harriette's eyes had widened at this news of perhaps having her son live overseas for a while longer but Eddie didn't seem to notice and it was then Felix realised that while Harriette had lived the majority of the past twenty-two years for her son, she had also let Eddie go so he could find his own life. That took courage, especially as they were so close. He remembered her elation at seeing Eddie at the airstrip. How would she cope when Eddie left?

A few days later, when Eddie started to book his flights back to France, stopping in America for a few days in order to break the long journey, Felix noticed that Harriette started to withdraw slightly. She was her usual happy self but the laughter in her eyes dimmed faster. At the hospital, he'd watch as she just stared out into space for a minute or two, completely lost in thought until someone asked her a question. The hugs she gave Eddie seemed to be longer and more intense.

'He'll be fine,' Felix murmured as she stood bravely on the edge of the airstrip and watched as her son boarded the small plane that would take him to Brisbane. From Brisbane, he'd head overseas, every step of his journey taking him further and further away from his mother.

'I know. I raised him to be fine, to cope, to enjoy his experiences.' Harriette's voice hitched in her throat as she waved again and blew kisses. Eddie blew kisses back and then disappeared inside. The stairs were pulled up and locked in place. Harriette looked at the windows, laughing when she could see Eddie making funny faces.

The laughter, however, didn't stop the tears from rolling down her cheeks and Felix found himself putting a soothing arm around her shoulders in an effort to support her.

He'd debated whether or not to bring Chloe with them but Harriette and Eddie had both said that if she saw Eddie get on the plane and leave, then she wouldn't be worried about where he'd gone. 'Especially with her parents just disappearing from her life, it's best if she can see that Eddie is OK and not…you know—'

'Dead?' he'd offered and she'd nodded.

'Then she can join in my online Internet chats with him so she can again see that he's all right.'

So he stood there now, his arm around Harriette's shoulders and his other hand holding onto Chloe's as she waved enthusiastically at Eddie and laughed along with Harriette at the funny faces Eddie was making.

That night, he watched as Harriette started to prepare dinner, noticing the slight slump of her shoulders. Felix knew he was supposed to be running Chloe's bath but the little girl was busy chatting away quietly to her toys, especially Captain Gumleaf.

'Can I help you with anything?' he asked Harriette, but she shook her head and sniffed before turning to look at him.

'I'm fine. Thanks.'

'Really?' Felix walked over and put a hand on her shoulder, wanting to comfort her but not entirely sure what was acceptable under the terms of their friendship. What he wanted was to turn her around and haul her into his arms, to wrap his own arms around her and let her wet the front of his cotton shirt with her tears. Even the thought of having a woman cry on him was so unlike him, so unlike the firm, staid and determined surgeon he'd been for so many years. Was it Chloe who had started to first break down those barriers or Harriette? Perhaps it was a combination of both.

'Harriette, he'll be fine.'

'I know. I know he will be, but until he calls me and tells me he's landed in Brisbane and then that he's in the States and then, in a few days' time, that he's back in Paris, then I have the right to worry.' She put down the knife she'd been using to chop the carrots.

'Of course you do.'

'This is what I wanted for him. I wanted him to

have all the experiences I couldn't have because by the time I was twenty-two, I had a six-year-old son, was working twenty hours a week as an orderly at the hospital and studying medicine the rest of the time. And I know that was my choice but it was hard and exhausting and I was often so stressed that I would get sick but Eddie was there, helping me, carrying my books, making me a cup of tea, doing more than usual six-year-olds because he had to.' Tears of determination were running down her cheeks as she continued. 'I worked hard so that he could have every opportunity, that he could have money for his first overseas trip, that he could have an amazing set of chef knives, that he was eligible for the scholarship. I did everything I could and now he's living his dreams and I love him for it but, oh, Felix, my heart aches so badly when he's not with me.'

The way she looked at him, the way her heart seemed to really be breaking because she was without her son, tugged at his own heart and then, without even thinking further about it, he found himself reaching for her and enveloping her in his arms. She went willingly, burying her face in her hands as she leant against his chest.

'He's my boy. My little boy.' The words came out as sobs. 'I love seeing him, spending time with him, but I hate it when he has to go, but I know he has to, because he has his own life and I have mine and I worked hard to become a doctor so that when the time came for him to leave me, to walk his own path, I wasn't left alone with no purpose in life. He knows that. He understands and…' Her words trailed off and she allowed the sorrow of having said goodbye to her adult son to overwhelm her.

Felix found himself rubbing one hand slowly up and down her back, offering comfort. The fact that he was enjoying the opportunity to be there for her was something he was going to regard as a privilege. He'd breathed in her sweet, summery scent many times before and it had never failed to have a hypnotic effect on him.

Her body was warm against his, soft and cuddly, and he couldn't deny he liked the way she felt in his arms. It was the oddest thing, allowing himself to admit to such emotions where he usually kept his distance, kept everyone at arm's length, yet with Harriette Jones he was definitely enjoying every moment. He didn't enjoy her pain or the grief at having to say goodbye to her son, but he was pleased she was allowing him to help her.

'It doesn't make any difference how old they are,' she mumbled, shifting her hands slightly away from her face and resting them onto his chest, her face still buried so he found it difficult to properly understand her. 'Whether they're Chloe's age or Eddie's age. Not being with them is the thing that eats away at a parent's heart.'

'Harriette.' Her name escaped from his lips, barely a whisper, and he closed his eyes and rested his chin atop her head, shifting so she was settled more comfortably in his arms. Her tears had stopped and she was now sniffing and hiccupping a little but her breathing was starting to even out. 'You really wear your emotions on your sleeve, don't you, Dr Jones?' he murmured and immediately felt her tense up. She pushed against his arms but he wasn't quite ready to let her go. 'No. No, Harriette, you misunderstood me. That's a good thing. I'm saying that's a good thing because I find it so incredibly difficult to—'

He stopped talking then because she'd lifted her head and was looking up at him with the utmost confusion. Her eyes were puffy, her cheeks were blotchy, her nose was red and her lips...her perfect, ready-to-kiss lips, were plump and parted and definitely ready for him to kiss.

CHAPTER EIGHT

HARRIETTE WASN'T SURE what was happening. She seemed to be frozen in place, looking up into Felix's handsome face. She'd noticed, all too often lately, how he combed his fingers through his hair when he was confused. She'd noticed how he was smiling more and more and how that smile had the ability to make her heart skip a beat. Plus, she'd most definitely noticed the growing awareness between the two of them. Naturally, she'd done her best to ignore it, and while Eddie had been here the goal had been easier to achieve, but now that her son was gone, she couldn't help feeling vulnerable.

She knew Felix wasn't taking advantage of the situation because, even though she'd been upset, she'd been able to see the struggle within him, to comfort or not to comfort and that was all he was offering. Although there might be a physical attraction buzzing beneath the surface, she knew it could never go anywhere because his attention needed to be on Chloe. The attraction was only the result of spending too much time together because ever since he'd arrived in Meeraji Lake, they'd been hard pressed to avoid each other. He needed her help, he needed her to be a friend, to help guide him through the parenting forest, knowing when to chop down a few trees to make something new and when to plant some saplings so that something beautiful would grow in years to come.

She drew in a deep, shaky breath and instantly realised her error in doing so. Where the deep breath was supposed to relax her, help her to get under control, all it did was alert her heightened senses to Felix's earthy scent. It was as though it contained a hint of spice and all things nice and it would be far too easy for her to stay right where she was and absorb everything else about the man. Comfort was one thing, but she shouldn't take advantage of his good nature. He was being nice, he was being a friend, and here she was, momentarily forgetting about why she'd been upset in the first place, her thoughts and tingling senses far too focused on the way his closeness was affecting her.

As though she could no longer remain in his arms under false pretences, she tried to pull back a little more, to break the embrace of his arms holding her tight, but Felix didn't seem to want to let her go. She gazed more closely into his perfect eyes, surprised by what she saw. Repressed desire! Felix desired her? The realisation made her mouth go dry and her heart beat, which had just started to settle to a more normal rhythm, picked up the pace again, although this time it wasn't because she was missing her son. In fact, right now she was glad Eddie wasn't here because the tension that was winding itself around herself and Felix was one of mutual awareness and need. She couldn't even put a name to what she was feeling but, whatever it was, it was something she hadn't felt in an incredibly long time.

But she couldn't. He was her colleague…her colleague with a very firm chest. Her colleague with a delicious spicy scent. Her colleague who was looking at her as though she were the most beautiful woman in the world?

How could he possibly look at her in such a

way? Stare at her mouth as though it were perfect? Gaze into her eyes as though he could drown in them? Send out those 'come closer' signals she was picking up on loud and clear?

He wanted to kiss her? Felix wanted to kiss her! The urge was clearly visible in his expressive eyes. The question remained: did she want to kiss him? Harriette had tried desperately not to move her hands, not to allow her itching fingers to spread out and touch his solid chest. She kept them as still as possible because even if she made the slightest movement, the shockwaves of delight at being able to touch him, to explore every contour of his perfectly formed body would—

'Harriette.' Had he spoken her name or had he thought it and she'd somehow tapped into his thoughts?

'Felix?' She tried to whisper his name, confusion evident in her tone, but she hiccupped a little as she spoke, her breath hitching a few times before she sighed and relaxed some more. It was far too easy to relax within his arms, those firm bands surrounding her as though he were never going to let her go. Part of her wished he wouldn't.

'Harriette,' he returned, his gaze flicking between her lips and her eyes. This time she knew he'd spoken her name because she hadn't been able to remove her gaze from his mouth, from watching it move, as though in slow motion, to speak her name. *Her* name. He was saying *her* name and causing her body to ignite with suppressed desire.

The hands at her back started to move in little circles, which only made pure fire spread throughout her entire body, bringing her dormant senses to life. He bent his elbows, then shifted his hands, bringing them up to cup her face. The instant his fingers touched her face, she sighed audibly at the delight he was invoking. Felix was as aware of her as she was of him and she couldn't help but lean a little into his right hand, wanting him to know that she felt whatever it was he was feeling, that it was reciprocated, that she wanted…she wanted…

'Harriette.' Again her name was soft and gentle on his lips, his parted lips, his parted lips that really weren't that far away from her own. They were so close that if she stood on tiptoe and leaned forward a little she…they… 'Why are you looking at me that way?'

She eased back, trying not to feel as though she'd been slapped in the face with his words. 'What way? I wasn't looking at you—' She stopped because she realised she was speaking quickly, too quickly, and that her voice was high pitched for some reason, as though she had something to hide. Had she read his expression incorrectly? Had she been on the verge of making a complete fool of herself? 'I'm not looking at you any particular way. Why would I do that? I wouldn't.' Her words were still too fast, filled with defensiveness. She shook her head a little, then closed her eyes in the hope that blocking him from her view might actually assist with calming her over-flustered senses into some state of normal. 'I was just…I was upset and you offered me—'

Harriette felt his finger land on her lips to stop her from babbling and she quickly opened her eyes and stared at him. There was the slight hint of mirth in his expression but also awareness. 'Let me rephrase that.' He slowly removed his finger from her lips, then rested his hand on her neck, the other one still cupping her face. 'What I meant to say was, why are you looking at me in such a way that makes me want to kiss you?'

'You want to—' She stopped, unable to finish her sentence as the embarrassment she'd felt only seconds ago was replaced by an overwhelming sense of wanting, of needing, of being desperate to feel as she hoped only Felix could make her feel. Her heart rate increased, every sense within her body seemed to tingle with utter delight and all because Felix wanted to…wanted to…

'Kiss you,' he finished for her. 'Yes.'

'Oh.' Clearly they were now openly acknowledging the attraction that had been building slowly between them. Harriette continued to stare at him, quite unsure what to do next. 'Uh…this may surprise you,' she eventually babbled, her words just as fast as before, 'but…um…I have no idea what to do next.'

Felix raised his eyebrows in surprise at her statement but then smiled. 'Do you mean kissing? Or just…in general?'

Harriette shifted a little, feeling highly self-conscious, but all her movements did was to highlight that her hands were still against Felix's chest, splayed out over his shirt, the cotton fibres doing little to disguise his excellent male physique beneath. At the contact, it was as though jolts of heat radiated up each finger and thumb before travelling up her arms and then bursting throughout her body in a frenzied rush of fireworks.

'Allow me to help you with that,' he murmured, and the next thing she realised was that his head was descending towards her own, their breath beginning to mingle, the faintest touch of their lips against each other. If she'd thought there had been fireworks bursting throughout her body before, it was nothing compared to now.

The kiss was soft, testing, tentative, as though neither of them were sure this was the right thing to do but simply couldn't resist any longer. Self-control, it seemed, had taken a momentary vacation but she wasn't complaining.

Felix was kissing her. He was holding her and he was kissing her. He wanted to kiss her. He was clearly enjoying it as the next touch against her lips was firmer than the one before. Nothing mattered at the moment. Not their patients, their living arrangements, their families. It was just the two of them, together...kissing.

He was awakening dormant emotions, making her feel things she hadn't felt in an incredibly long time and...and...her mind was starting to shut down all avenues of logical thought as her heart opened, as butterflies swirled in her mind, as emotions of delight and happiness and lightness and unexpected pleasure coursed through her.

Even when Felix pulled back, resting his forehead against her own, both of them basking in the soft and tantalising wake of having satisfied temptation, Harriette still found it difficult to believe she wasn't dreaming, that this was actually happening.

Felix was talking to her, speaking words of some kind, but her mind was busy wondering if he wanted to repeat the action, but this time to go a little further, to increase the intensity of the kiss rather than keeping it controlled and testing.

At that particular moment, it didn't matter she'd previously told herself she wasn't interested in any sort of relationship with any man because she had far too many other important things to be doing. When the reality of a warm-blooded male who found her attractive was actually staring her in the face, it caused the box in her mind that she'd labelled do not open to open wide and fill her with longing. A longing for companionship, a longing for intimacy but, most of all, a longing for acceptance.

'What do you think?' Felix asked her softly. 'It's the right thing to do. For all of us.'

'Wait.' She shifted back a touch, doing her level best to ignore his warmth, to ignore the sensual pheromones swirling around them, and looked at him. 'I'm sorry. Would you mind saying all that again, please?' She almost added, 'Because I have trouble concentrating when you're this close,' but, thankfully, she stopped herself in time. If Felix was saying what she thought he was saying, the more she guarded her own heart, the better. She'd been heartbroken before and she wasn't going to allow herself to be that vulnerable ever again.

'I said that while this is great, kissing you and wanting to kiss you some more...' He paused and cleared his throat. 'I'm not convinced this is the right time—for you, for me, for Chloe and—'

Harriette instantly dropped her hands back to her sides and stepped away from him, bumping into the bench and hurting her hip.

'Are you OK?' he asked, reaching out a caring hand. She held hers up in defence and side-stepped him, ignoring the pain coursing up and down her right leg.

'I'm fine. Fine. Absolutely fine and dandy.'

'Harriette,' he tried as she walked the long way around the kitchen table in order to get into the lounge room because from where she'd stood, he'd been blocking her exit.

'It's fine, Felix. You're absolutely correct. Even though we may feel an attraction, it's no doubt only because of our close living and working situation plus the fact that we're both helping Chloe, and that's good that your focus is on Chloe. It should be on Chloe and it is so how could I possibly argue with that? Even if I was going to argue, which I'm not because I agree with you. Good decision.' The entire time she'd been talking, she'd walked backwards into the lounge room where Chloe was starting to get bored playing with her toys. 'In fact, it looks as though she needs you now and I should head over to the clinic to finish off some paperwork and—' She stopped and, without bothering to finish her sentence, turned and headed to her bedroom, closing the door firmly behind her.

How could she have been so stupid? How could she have imagined that anything good could ever happen to her? That any man would love and desire her for who she was, no matter what was going on around them. Logically she knew he'd made the right call but, emotionally, the sensation of loneliness swept over her. She should never have allowed that box to open, the box that contained her most intimate wants and desires.

She dragged in a breath. She'd been caught up in the moment. That was all. The box could be shut again and shoved back on the shelf. She could ignore it, just as she had for the past few decades. Harriette knew Felix's first priority had to be Chloe. She, more than anyone, should realise that the child always came first when one was a single parent, and therefore she couldn't fault Felix's reasoning, nor could she hold anything against him. He'd been open and honest with her. How could she fault that? How?

Harriette could feel another bout of tears beginning to rise within her. Loneliness. It had already swamped her once today with Eddie's departure and now she also had to face the prospect that she would always be alone in this world. Yes, she had Eddie but his own life would begin to take up more of his time. He would eventually find a partner, have children of his own, keep pursuing his career, and her role in his life would become even more diminished than ever before and that was when she could give herself up to loneliness. She laughed without humour, remembering how, when Eddie had been little, all she'd wanted was a few hours of alone time, to be by herself, to watch a movie or read a book. It had been her saving grace, that alone time, and now, when she was looking towards her future, all she saw was alone time.

She'd told herself that she didn't want to go down the family road again. She wasn't interested in having more children, and when she'd dated in the past it had been with professional colleagues who were focused on their careers, but even then she'd found them two-dimensional given they didn't have strong family connections to balance them out. That was probably how Felix would have been if Chloe hadn't been thrust upon him. He would have been two-dimensional and even if she had been attracted to him, which, given the way he looked, would have been a definite, she still would have found him two-dimensional. Now, though, seeing him interact with Chloe, making the effort to get to know his niece, to become a permanent fixture in her life, she found him far more attractive. He was changing, learning, accepting and offering love to a child who needed it. What woman wouldn't be attracted to him?

Even though she'd told herself no more children, no more distractions, tonight, for one split second, she'd allowed herself to dream, to see a future with a tall handsome man and his little girl. The images had flashed through her mind like a series of instant photographs and, for one split second, hope had flared strong and firm within her heart, before it was quashed once more.

She closed her eyes and listened, hearing his deep tones mixing with Chloe's higher-pitched ones, both of them laughing. Oh, how it warmed her heart to hear him having a good time with his niece, especially when Chloe still didn't seem too sure of him at times. At least the child was starting to view Uncle Felix in a different light and lo and behold the gift of a tea set had been the avenue to allow that to happen.

She opened her eyes and walked to the mirror on her dresser, looking at her reflection. Good heavens, she really did look a mess. Her hair was more of a bird's nest than normal, her eyes were puffy and her nose was red. And Felix had seen her looking like this? No wonder he'd decided to focus on Chloe rather than pursuing an attraction with a woman who looked as if she'd just been put through the wringer.

Quietly, Harriette opened her bedroom door and headed to the bathroom where she splashed water on her face and added a bit of make-up. She fixed her hair, wrapping it into a loose bun on her head, several tendrils still escaping the bonds because they were too short to stay secured without clips.

'At least it's a bit of an improvement,' she told her reflection and, after taking a few deep breaths, she walked quickly though the house, trying to ignore the sight of Felix lounging on the floor with Chloe near him, the two of them looking at pictures from one of her books. 'Off to clinic,' she murmured, heading straight for the door.

Pasting on a bright smile, she headed into the clinic, greeting her waiting patients with her usual optimism and joviality. She listened to them, prescribed treatments for them and wrote up her clinic notes. Once she was done, she headed to the hospital to touch base with her patients on the ward and to check with Tori that the ED was running smoothly.

'No emergencies,' the nurse reported. 'I've just finished restocking all the rooms and writing out an order form for next month.'

'Sound like fun times.' Harriette sat down in the seat next to her friend and sighed.

'How are you coping?'

'What?' Could Tori read her expression that well? Could she see the feelings for Felix? How could the nurse possibly know what had transpired between the two doctors?

'It can't be easy saying goodbye to him.'

'Eddie!' Harriette breathed a sigh of relief. 'No, it's not easy but I raised a good boy and he

LUCY CLARK   191

knows to contact his neurotic mother the instant he lands.'

Tori looked at her quizzically for a moment. 'What did you think I meant?'

'Nothing. My mind was on the patients I've just seen at clinic.' She waggled a finger near her head. 'How are the wedding preparations going?' She needed to change the subject and fast and what bride-to-be could resist talking about her up-and-coming wedding?

As Tori talked about her latest wedding drama Harriette silently chided herself for having misinterpreted the question. She needed to stop fixating on what had almost happened between herself and Felix.

'Are you and Felix still planning to stop in at Darwin after the house calls?' Tori's question caught Harriette a little off guard and she knocked over a container full of pens at the mention of Felix.

'What?'

'The house calls? You told me you wanted to go to Darwin once you've done the house clinics. It does seem quite logical. You're already going to be working your way up further into the Northern Territory so why not go a little further and show Felix and Chloe a bit of the closest capital city? I'm presuming Felix hasn't been to Darwin before?'

'Not that I know of.' She shook her head, forgetting the planning she'd already made for their trip. 'We leave the day after tomorrow.' Harriette couldn't keep the doom and gloom from her tone. She'd organised it while Eddie had been here and she'd been looking forward to helping Felix mend the fences with his father. Now…now she didn't want to be cooped up in a car with Felix for an extended period of time. And after they'd finished in Darwin, they would be spending three days driving back to Meeraji Lake, stopping and doing district clinics on the way. If she'd thought they were living and working in close quarters now, then it would be nothing compared to the way they'd be forced together during the next week.

Tori chuckled. 'Cheer up. It's not as though it's any great hardship being in such close quarters with Felix. He is one good-looking man… but nowhere near as good-looking as my fantastic fiancé, who is presently walking in the front doors.' The nurse waved to Scotty and went to embrace him.

After offering a brief g'day to Scotty, Harriette headed to the wards to check on her patients, but even as she paid them the attention they deserved thoughts of Felix remained in the back of her mind. She decided to try and do some paperwork as that usually required her full concentration, but it didn't work.

If only they hadn't kissed! What had they been thinking? Well, that was the problem— they hadn't been. They'd given in to temptation and now she had to pay the price, the price of being uncomfortable in his company. Harriette sat alone in her small office and buried her head in her hands as misery, discomfort and loneliness swamped her. 'What am I supposed to do?' she mumbled into the silent room.

She stopped her thoughts and shook her head. A week with Felix, in a car, driving from homestead to homestead and then ending up in Darwin for one night before starting the drive back to Meeraji Lake. It would be so confining, so uncomfortable and yet incredibly intimate. Thank goodness Chloe was going with them. At least the almost-four-year-old would break the tension...or so Harriette hoped. Getting through the next week was going to require her utmost concentration and professionalism because there was no way she was going to let Felix McLaren lure her into such a confused situation again.

Harriette straightened her shoulders, determination coursing through her. She could do this. She'd managed to navigate her way through situations far more difficult than this one. Then again, she hadn't been faced with a man who made her heart race, her knees go weak and her body fill with desire just by smiling at her.

Her shoulders sagged. It was hopeless.

CHAPTER NINE

'ARE WE THERE YET?'

Chloe's voice from the back seat of the four-door utility truck made Harriette smile. She concentrated on driving while Felix turned and addressed the little girl. The rear of the vehicle was packed with everything they would need to hold travelling clinics for the next few days, along with clothes for the three of them and an entire bag of 'stuff' for Chloe, which she'd insisted upon bringing with her. Captain Gumleaf, of course, was sitting in the back with her, strapped into his own seatbelt to make sure he was safe.

'It's only ten minutes since you last asked.' He grinned at her. 'Would you like a drink?'

Chloe screwed up her nose. 'Will I have to go to the toilet in the bush again?'

Harriette chuckled and looked in her rear-vision mirror, reflecting on the look of horror on Chloe's face when they'd had to stop a few hours ago so the child could relieve herself behind one of the native shrubs that was scattered here and there along the way. To say Chloe hadn't been impressed was an understatement. 'There is a good chance that may happen, Chloe, depending on how much you drink.'

'I don't like doing that,' Chloe stated and shook her head as Felix held out her drink bottle.

'You've got to drink, Chloe.' His tone was caring but insistent.

'I don't want to!' She sat in her car seat and crossed her arms with determination, a frown on her face, her little lips puckered in defiance.

Harriette laughed again and Felix turned on her. 'What's so funny? She's got to drink. Out here in the Australian outback, it's imperative to remain hydrated, especially when in a car. The heat outside is—'

'The car is air-conditioned, so we're hardly at risk of overheating, and she's already drunk quite a bit today. I don't blame her about not wanting to urinate in the bushes. It's far easier for you males than us females and, to make my final point, we're only about forty-five minutes away from arriving at the first homestead. Once we're there, she'll eat and drink and urinate in a proper toilet.' She looked over her shoulder and winked at Chloe. 'Isn't that right, princess?' she stated rhetorically.

'Proper loo,' Chloe repeated, naturally translating the word into her English counterpart. She uncrossed her arms and clapped her hands. 'Proper loo.'

'At least she's smiling, now,' Harriette remarked as Felix scowled at her. 'You look just like Chloe,' she said, teasing him slightly. 'All frowny and grumpy.'

'I'm not grumpy,' he stated. 'I'm annoyed. There's a difference.' Without another word, he pressed the button for the CD to start playing, pleased that Erica had given them quite a few different children's CDs for Chloe to listen to on the long drives.

'I've already heard this one,' she stated from the back.

'And now you can hear it again,' he retorted, seemingly annoyed with both the females. He waited a few minutes, until he could hear Chloe singing along with the song, then shifted in his seat so he was facing Harriette. 'I don't appreciate the way you're constantly undermining my authority with Chloe,' he remarked, doing his best to keep his tone level so Chloe couldn't hear him. He'd noticed that the little girl often picked up on undercurrents between Harriette and himself and ended up having tantrums over it, as though thinking that if the two main adults in her life were misbehaving, it was perfectly all right for her to do so as well.

That was the way it had been in the house until they'd left for this trip. He wouldn't say that he and Harriette had had tantrums, per se, but the atmosphere certainly hadn't been one of relaxed joviality as it had been before they'd kissed. Harriette's attitude had been one of polite indifference. She'd arranged to eat out at different friends' houses, saying that she'd neglected her friends while Eddie had been here. That had meant cheese sandwiches for Chloe and a tin of soup for him as he hadn't felt much like cooking. After Eddie's gourmet cooking, his soup had tasted bland and unappetising and he'd kept glancing at the door every time he'd heard a sound, hoping it was Harriette coming home to spend some time with them.

She hadn't. Not at least until rather late into the evening when he'd bathed Chloe and wrangled her to sleep. And when she had come in, she'd walked straight past him, murmured a polite goodnight and headed to her part of the house.

Felix knew Harriette had every right to go and see her friends—after all, the two of them were just colleagues, or at least that was the way she was making him feel. He'd thought they'd progressed past that, that they'd become friends as well. They had, he realised, until they'd kissed and everything had changed.

'I'm sorry,' she replied, bringing his thoughts back to the present. 'I guess it's the mother in me that takes over.'

'I know you know more than I do, but how am I supposed to learn if you keep jumping in and contradicting what I say?'

'I wasn't contradicting—not really. I was…justifying and explaining to her. She has every right to say she doesn't want to go to the toilet in the bushes, even though out here it's almost considered a rite of passage.' Harriette grinned, the ute still speeding along on the endlessly straight road with not a house in sight. 'Still, I will do my best to refrain from appearing to undermine your authority because it *is* important for you to exert it.'

'And you'll try to back off? To let me at least attempt to deal with Chloe on my own?'

'I'll most certainly try and bite my tongue, but only on the condition that if you need help with Chloe, if you feel out of your depth, you'll ask me for help or advice. I can't promise I'll always know what to do but we can work it out together.'

'Can we?' The two words were softer than the others and the tone in them had definitely changed. A prickle of apprehension washed over Harriette, and when she risked a glance at him again it was to find him watching her more intently than before. Clearly they weren't talking about Chloe any more.

'Of course we can,' she remarked, keeping her tone as jovial as possible.

'You like children, don't you?'

For a second, she thought she'd misinterpreted what he was saying. Was this going to become a habit? Was she ever going to be able to figure him out, figure out his moods, or was she always going to be grabbing the wrong end of the stick? 'Uh...of course I do.'

'Would you like to have more?'

This time she turned her head and stared at him for a long moment. 'Me? More children!' He nodded. 'No. No. No.' She shook her head and returned her attention to the boring, very straight road. 'I mean, could you imagine it? Having my kids over two decades apart? That's a bit… strange.' She laughed, then shook her head again. 'It would be funny to see Eddie's face when I told him I was having another child but—no. I've worked too hard for too long to finish my surgical training and I'm so close to being finished.'

'You can have career and family, you know.'

'Like you? How's your career going since Chloe entered your life?'

Felix thought for a moment before agreeing. 'Point taken.' He eased back into the chair as they drove along and Harriette refocused her attention on the road. 'What about men?'

'Pardon?' She stared at him again, wondering if she'd heard him correctly.

'Have you ever had a serious relationship? I mean, apart from Eddie's father.'

'Uh…sort of. I've dated colleagues in the past

and not really seriously until Eddie was in his teens.'

'Fair enough, but none made you want to take a trip down the aisle? Have more kids?'

Harriette frowned as she drove along, pleased she had the protection of her sunglasses as she answered his questions. 'I was serious about one guy. Eddie was seventeen, hanging out with his mates and being hormonally obnoxious.'

'Eddie? Hormonally obnoxious?' He chuckled.

'Happens to all of us,' she added, smiling at him.

'So…the guy?' Felix prompted when she remained silent for a moment.

'Right. The guy. His name was Mark and he had moved to the country to work in the hospital for a few years. I was deciding whether or not to specialise in surgery and he just seemed to make my life so much richer. He supported me in my career, he was great with Eddie and everything seemed perfect.'

'And then?'

'And then he had articles published in a reputed journal and was offered a fellowship.'

'Wait. Not Mark Masters?'

Harriette snorted with derision. 'One and the same. Clearly you know him.'

'I took over the fellowship from him.'

'Of course you did.' And there it was in a nutshell. Felix might be putting Chloe first, but his career still came second, which meant there really wasn't any room in his life for Harriette. 'All you career-climbing surgeons know each other.'

'So I take it he left the country hospital for the high life?'

'In the middle of his contract, leaving me shortstaffed and overworked. Eddie was devastated.'

'As were you, I'm sure.'

Harriette could only shrug, and before he could ask her any more personal questions she turned up the music a little and began singing along with Chloe.

'Let me know if you're becoming fatigued and I'll take over,' he offered ten minutes later.

'It's not long now and, besides, I'm used to driving long distances.'

'How often are these clinics?'

Although they'd already been over this once, it was clear Felix needed to get a full grasp on the strange situation of taking the doctor to the patients rather than the other way around. 'Once a month. Depending on how many clinics are being held, usually one of us goes out and the other stays in Meeraji Lake.'

'But now that we're both going, Tori and the rest of the staff are holding down the fort? What if an emergency comes in?'

'Generally, because people know we're holding district clinics, they'll travel to the homestead where the clinic is being held. Usually it's closer for them than coming into town.'

'And these clinics are held because a lot of outback people can't, or won't, take time off to visit the doctor even when they're sick?'

'Yes. Outback Australians are made of sturdy stuff and sometimes they think they're immortal. These clinics mean more people can be immunised, especially for things like tetanus, and have their concerns addressed without needing to take a day or two off work in order to drive to Meeraji Lake.' She was starting to slow the vehicle down. He still couldn't see anything around them apart from the odd tree and shrub and a lot of reddish-brown dirt so he wasn't sure why she was slowing down.

'Where are we going?' he asked as she turned the vehicle onto what could only be described as a dirt track.

'To the homestead. This is a shortcut.'

'Shortcut? Are you sure that's wise?'

Harriette laughed at him. 'We can go the long way around and add another hour to our journey?'

'No. No. This way is good.' Felix held onto the hand grip above the passenger door as the utility truck made its way over ground that appeared to be flat but was in fact rather undulating. He checked Chloe in the back but she seemed perfectly fine with the new terrain. In fact, she was clapping her hands with joy at the bumps and giggling. 'Great. She's a daredevil, just like David.'

Harriette laughed again and continued navigating their way across country. Twenty minutes later, she turned onto a graded gravel road and soon after that she turned into what could only be described as a long dirt driveway, the sign at the turn-off to the homestead the only indication that this was the correct way.

'You'll have to jump out and open and close the gates for me,' she told him, and as he did as she asked Harriette had to admit that the day's driving adventures hadn't been as bad as she'd initially thought. She'd anticipated that it would have been confining in the small cabin of the truck, that Felix's scent would drive her crazy and that the close proximity would be distracting but, in actual fact, she'd enjoyed it. Her embarrassment at having been a fool in his arms a few days ago had decreased and she'd managed to return her spirits to her usual jovial self.

Harriette brought the vehicle to a stop outside the front of the homestead, a lot of cars already parked, people milling around ready and waiting for the afternoon clinic to begin.

'What's all this?' Felix looked out of the window at the plethora of people.

'Patients.'

'I hadn't expected this many. It's like a week's worth of clinic hours all in one hit.'

She grinned. 'Busier than a major hospital, mate.' She switched off the engine and removed the key from the ignition before jumping out of the car and waving to the owner of the homestead. Remembering their earlier conversation about how Felix needed to be the parent with

Chloe, she left it up to him to get the child from the car and, instead, Harriette went to say hello to some of the locals she hadn't yet met.

Surrounded by people, they unpacked their belongings from the ute and headed inside where their hosts had set up rooms for a makeshift clinic.

'What do I do with Chloe?' Felix asked as Harriette handed him a note pad and pen so he could write down notes on each patient. She was opening the medical kits and other equipment they'd brought with them, such as tongue depressors, gloves and an array of bandages.

'I think she's already playing with the other children out the back in the sandpit.' Harriette finished setting things up for him before heading next door into her own consulting room to do the same.

'But how do I know she's going to be supervised properly? What if she decides to run away out here?' Felix had followed her, clearly anxious.

'Then you'd best go talk to her, set down some guidelines and find out who's in charge of looking after the children and let Chloe know.' Harriette could quite easily have taken over but that wasn't the way for Felix to learn. 'Communication, in any relationship, is paramount.'

'Right. Right. Good. Talk to Chloe. I can do that. Thanks,' he returned, and as he disappeared from her view she couldn't help but smile at the progress he'd made in such a short time. At least now he was more than willing to talk to Chloe, to interact with the little girl and to ensure that her safety came first.

'Doc?' There was a knock at her open door and when she looked up it was to find a man in his late thirties standing there with an old towel wrapped around his hand. 'I've just arrived and the blokes outside said I could jump the queue.'

Harriette nodded and ushered him in, closing the door. Clinic time had clearly begun whether she liked it or not, and as she unwrapped the towel she discovered a fencing nail going into the man's hand.

'Here we go,' she whispered beneath her breath as she gathered together the supplies she would need. She treated her patient, giving him a local anaesthetic before removing the nail. She debrided the wound and then packed and dressed it.

'You'll need to have the dressing changed regularly for the next three weeks. I'll put you on the district nurses' roster but when they can't make it to you, you'll either need to get to Meeraji Lake or to Darwin.' Harriette tried to smother a yawn as she spoke.

'You all right, Doc?'

'Just a bit tired from driving this morning. It'll settle down.' She started to write up the case notes for her patient, then asked him to send in the next person.

'How are you going?' Harriette asked Felix a few hours later as they stopped for a drink of cool iced tea.

'Getting through them. There's such a variety of problems. I hadn't expected that.'

She clinked her glass with his and grinned. 'Far more exciting than your average hospital clinic, right?'

Felix pondered her words for a moment, which only made her smile increase. 'What are you smiling at?' he asked, giving her that cute little quizzical smile.

'You.'

'What about me?'

'You like to really ponder things before you speak or make a decision and that's great.'

He nodded and leaned on the kitchen bench as a few of the older kids who were around the place came hurtling through. Harriette stepped forward in order to get out of the way and when she next looked at Felix, she realised just how close they were. 'And you, Harriette, like to say whatever it is that comes into your mind.'

'Hey. I do think things through. Perhaps I just think faster than you.'

He angled his head to the side and regarded her for a moment; she wished he hadn't, especially as his gaze dipped to take in the shape of her mouth, lingering there a second too long before returning to look into her eyes. Didn't he realise how he was affecting her? How that long look had brought a mass of tingles to flood through her body, had caused a wanting heat to wash over her?

She tried to return her thoughts to an even keel, to ignore the way he was making her feel. Theirs was a relationship that would remain professional and platonic, with her helping him to learn how to parent Chloe. She could accept that, but if she was to get through the rest of this year, working alongside Felix, living in the same house as him, seeing him become a wonderful father—as she'd already glimpsed—then she needed to find a way to keep her emotion under control. There would be countless more times when they would need to be this close, where the heat from their bodies would be combining together, where their scents would blend to become one heady concoction of desire.

She breathed out, trying not to look at his mouth but failing miserably, and what she saw there were his lips curved into a small smile. She looked at his eyes and saw one eyebrow raised in a teasing but very interested manner.

'You were saying?'

'Uh…' Harriette tried desperately to think of what she'd been saying, of what her last thought was, but all she could remember was how much she wanted him to kiss her again.

'You think faster than I do?' he continued to tease and she realised he knew full well that their present closeness was having a devastating effect on her equilibrium.

'Stop teasing me, Felix.' Her words were soft, intimate and meant only for him.

'Or what?' he challenged.

'Or I may shut you up by kissing you.'

His smile increased, which only disarmed her more. She'd half expected him to take a step back at her words, to put some distance between them, to become uncomfortable at her straightforward speaking. 'I can think of worse punishments,' he countered, his gaze once more dipping to take in her mouth.

Harriette sighed with repressed desire and clenched her jaw to stop herself from leaning forward and following through on her threat. 'Why are you doing this to me? You were the one who said we shouldn't get involved, that we needed to think of Chloe, that you didn't want me undermining—'

Felix placed a finger over her lips to stop her from talking, the touch causing her to gasp, the desire buzzing through her magnifying. 'Perhaps I was…a bit hasty. Perhaps we should—'

He broke off as the owner of the homestead came into the kitchen and he immediately dropped his hand but didn't ease back, still leaning casually on the bench. Harriette was the one to straighten, to take a step back, to try not looking guilty at being caught in an intimate tête-à-tête.

'Find everything you need?' Paulette asked them.

'Yes, thank you,' Felix answered as he took another sip of his long, cool drink. 'Harriette and I were just discussing a few of the patients,' he offered, as though explaining why they'd been standing so close. 'As this is my first outback homestead clinic, I needed to clarify a few things.'

'Fair enough,' Paulette responded. 'Now, I've had a few problems with people needing to stay the night and the fact is that I've run out of beds. Harriette, I had you and Chloe in the last room at the end of the corridor. There's a double bed in there but, Felix, I don't have anywhere for you to sleep. A lot of the men are dossing down in the lounge room but they've all got sleeping bags with them. Some are sleeping outside in their swags but at the moment the only real bed I have left is the one Harriette and Chloe will be sharing.'

'What?' It was Harriette who reacted. 'None of the couches are free?'

Paulette shook her head. 'I didn't think it right to assign poor Felix to a space on the floor or to a couch, given you've both got to do a clinic first thing in the morning, plus you've been driving. You're both going to be exhausted and—'

'It's no problem,' Felix stated, finishing his drink and taking the glass to stack in the dishwasher. 'Harriette and I can share with Chloe in the middle of us. She'll love that.' He smiled at Paulette. 'You're doing a great job dealing with the gaggle of people here.'

Paulette seemed taken aback at his praise and smiled warmly at him. 'Oh. Well, thank you.' She actually fanned her face. 'How lovely of you to say so.' She glanced at Harriette. 'I can see why he's considered the new catch of the county. Luckily I'm a happily married woman.'

Harriette drained her glass of its contents and went to put it into the dishwasher but Felix took it from her and performed the task. The last thing she wanted was to be discussing how Felix was bachelor of the year; to listen to the gossip that was no doubt already spread right around the district, especially when she'd been contemplating kissing him again.

'Right. Back to work.' With that, she left Felix and Paulette in the kitchen and called her next patient through into her makeshift consulting room. How she managed to get through the rest of the patients scheduled for that evening, she had no clue. With the way he'd looked at her in the kitchen, with the way he'd placed his finger over her lips, causing her breathing to increase and her senses to become even more heightened, it was enough to make her hyperventilate by just thinking about it.

How on earth was she supposed to sleep the entire night in the same bed as him? Of course, from a practical point of view, it was the best solution. They would both get to sleep on a comfortable mattress and awake refreshed in the morning, ready for the next clinic, but, to own the truth, being that close to Felix—all night long—especially with the way he was making her feel, meant she doubted she'd get any sleep whatsoever.

She could always go and sleep in the ute. It would be uncomfortable but she was sure she would actually get more shut-eye than she would being so close and yet so far from Felix. How was it that this man had somehow commandeered every aspect of her thoughts—except for the medical professional part? She'd managed to get her thoughts in order, to simply be colleagues with Felix, to be friendly but to keep her distance, to help him with Chloe. That was all she'd been planning to do for the next year and, hopefully, somewhere in the process of denying herself, she would find a level of compatibility with Felix where they could lose the awkward awareness of each other and achieve a companionable existence.

Not any more!

CHAPTER TEN

BY THE TIME the patients had all been seen and Paulette's husband had barbecued an enormous amount of food to feed those who had come for the clinic or were staying the night, Harriette had to admit she was exhausted.

People were still chatting and eating and drinking, some were leaving to head back to their homes, others were already asleep on the floor in their sleeping bags. With Chloe starting to look as though she would fall asleep at any given moment, Harriette picked the little girl up from where she'd been playing with one of her new friends, and carried her towards where Felix was chatting with a few of the patients he'd treated that day.

It was good to see him mixing with the locals where she'd half expected him to keep himself aloof, separate, superior. He watched her walk towards him, Chloe's head resting on her shoulder.

'Do you want me to take her?' he asked, putting his glass of iced tea down on a nearby table.

'It's fine. I'm happy to put her to bed tonight, if that's OK with you.'

A mild look of relief crossed his face and she realised that he hadn't wanted Chloe to have one of her tantrums when she was eventually put to bed. 'Thanks.'

That was all she needed, his permission—because there was no way she wanted to be accused of overstepping the mark once again. With a smile and a brief nod in his direction, Harriette headed back to the homestead, where she quickly brushed Chloe's teeth and then got her ready for bed, glad their bags had been put into the room. Once Chloe was settled, Harriette found herself yawning profusely and decided she would follow suit. She doubted anyone would miss her if she went to bed now. Besides, if she could fall asleep with Chloe before Felix came to bed, then she wouldn't have to think about him lying next to her.

After doing her teeth, changing into her pyjamas and plaiting her hair so it didn't get in the way, Harriette climbed between the cool sheets, the little girl instantly snuggling in and wrapping her arms around Harriette's neck. The action helped Harriette to relax, loving the sensation of having a child sleeping next to her. It reminded her of those times when Eddie had had bad dreams, or had just wanted to have a 'sleepover' in mummy's bed. Her little boy. Her precious little boy who was now such an incredible young man, but in her eyes he would be *her* little boy for ever.

Which was why she was astonished by the sensation of feeling as though Chloe were *her* little girl. Since they'd met, she'd been amazed with the way the child made her feel, heightening her dormant maternal instincts. She loved playing with the toys, reading the stories, engaging the imagination, especially during their tea parties. Even though Harriette had been focusing on her career, she'd been desperate to do that because she'd needed to ensure she had a life once Eddie had left her. Now that he was actually living on the other side of the world, she'd needed to surround herself with people, to become a part of a new community, but what she hadn't counted on was Felix.

Felix had changed everything. Not only had he brought Chloe into her life, but he'd raised dormant feelings, ones she hadn't expected to cope with. Before, when he'd been flirting with her in the kitchen, every sense in her body had been heightened and on red alert...alert in case he actually followed through on the desire she'd clearly seen in his eyes.

He was confusing her. He'd told her he didn't want to start a relationship with her and she'd respected his wishes, sorted her head out and decided to make this trip one of friendship and fun. Now, he was saying he'd made a mistake, that he *wanted* to see where things might lead...or was he? She had no idea because tomorrow he could change his mind again, if he so chose, and then where would she be?

'It's too confusing, Chloe,' she whispered to the sleeping child. 'I like him. I really do. I like him a lot. He makes me think, he makes me feel and he makes me want more for the life that I've tried to plan for myself.' Surprisingly, as she whispered the words into the dark quiet room, Harriette found her eyes starting to fill with tears.

'I wanted the "happily ever after" ending all

those years ago and I didn't get it, so I never let myself think about it again. I had Eddie and that was enough but now he's gone…he's gone, Chloe, he's left me, and…and…' She stopped, knowing there was no point in upsetting herself. If she allowed her thoughts to continue down this path, she would end up crying herself to sleep and no doubt wetting poor Chloe in the process. Deep down inside, Harriette had always wanted the normalcy of what society at large called 'a family'. Two parents raising children together.

'Little girl,' she continued to whisper after a moment, her words less broken than before. 'You have brought laughter and sunshine into my life.' And so has your uncle, she added silently, and as she listened to the child's even breathing Harriette found herself drifting off to sleep, thoughts of Felix mixing with her dreams, dreams of the two of them walking along hand in hand, teasing each other, working alongside each other at the hospital. She pictured not only herself and Felix, together, as a couple, but also with Chloe and Eddie, the four of them making up a mix-and-match of a family but a family nevertheless.

* * *

Felix had been well aware that when Harriette had gone to put Chloe to bed, she hadn't returned. He knew because he'd been looking for her, scanning the gathered group of people for a glimpse of her beautiful face. As he finally said his goodnights and went to the room assigned to them, he found exactly where Harriette had disappeared to.

How long he stood there by the bed, watching the two sleeping females who had become so important to him in such a short time, he had no idea. Chloe was lying on her back, one arm up above her head, the other almost across Harriette's face. Harriette lay on her side, one protective arm curled around the little girl, both of them breathing deeply. He wasn't at all surprised Harriette had been so exhausted, given that she'd driven the entire way to the homestead and then done a clinic on top of that.

She made a little noise, a little sighing sound and a small smile tugged at her lips. A buzz of protective desire flooded through him and he couldn't help recall the moment they'd shared in the kitchen earlier in the day. He'd wanted to kiss her again, wanted to see whether the chemistry from the first time had been a fluke or whether it was real. If it *was* the real deal, if his growing feelings towards Harriette continued to soar, what would happen then? His life had already been derailed once. Would it matter if it was derailed a second time?

The possibility of a different future, one he'd never considered before—a future of him, Chloe and Harriette, along with Eddie…together as a family—made him tremble with longing. He quickly turned away from the vision of loveliness in the bed and went to brush his teeth. When he returned and contemplated getting into the bed with Harriette so near and yet so far, he felt it better to sleep fully clothed. It was a warm night and he didn't really need covers so, instead, he lay down on top of the bed and tried to relax. He listened to Harriette's and Chloe's even breathing and slowly…very slowly, he drifted off to sleep as exhaustion caught up with him.

A loud scream of delight pierced Harriette's dream world and she woke with a start. 'Chloe!' Her eyes were wide open and every muscle in her body was tense. Chloe wasn't in the bed at all. In fact, no one was in the bed with her. She was all alone but she could see the dint Felix's head had made on the pillow, which indicated he had actually come in and slept. She didn't remember at all.

Harriette stared at the pillow for a second before picking it up and smelling it. Yes. It smelt like him, that spicy hypnotic scent that had often excited her senses. Realising she was being foolish, she returned the pillow and searched around for her cellphone in order to check the time.

She was still looking for her phone when the door to the room opened and Chloe came running in, clambering onto the bed and bouncing on her knees. 'Wake up. Wake up.'

'I'm awake,' Harriette told her, slipping one hand around the little girl and relaxing at seeing she was all right.

'Uncle Felix! She's awake!'

'Excellent,' he remarked as he came in behind Chloe carrying a tray of food. 'Sit up, Dr Jones, as breakfast is served.'

'We made breakfast for you.' Chloe was still

bouncing on the bed, clearly bursting with excitement.

'Well, Paulette and her husband did the cooking,' Felix clarified. 'But I put some food on a plate for you and made you a cup of tea.'

'I helped pour the juice,' Chloe stated as Felix lowered the tray onto Harriette's lap, telling Chloe gently to stop bouncing on the bed or the juice might spill. The child did as he asked. 'And I picked the flowers for you from the garden,' the little girl added, and Harriette smiled brightly at the thin-stemmed flowers that were really weeds but looked absolutely delightful in a small glass of water in the corner of her breakfast tray.

'I'm…I'm overwhelmed.' Harriette gazed up at Felix, who was standing beside her, grinning as excitedly as Chloe. The thought was incredibly touching and she could see it was heartfelt, which made it all the more special.

'What's that mean?' Chloe started to bounce again, but when she saw Harriette's juice start to wobble she instantly stopped. 'Oh, sorry.'

'It means that I'm happy,' Harriette clarified. 'Chloe, why don't you put on your purple shoes and go and play with some of the other children?'

'Really? I can go outside?'

'Remember your hat,' Harriette added and held the tray as Chloe scrambled off the bed and located her shoes. She quickly slipped them on and then accepted the hat Felix was holding out to her. 'Bye.' And she was out of the door.

'Oh, to have the energy of a child,' Felix stated as he came around the other side of the bed and sat down next to Harriette. When he didn't make any more effort to move, she turned her head and looked at him.

'Are you just going to sit there and watch me eat?'

'Yep.'

'Have you eaten?'

'Yep. Come on,' he urged. 'It's getting cold. Don't want Paulette's hard work cooking the bacon, eggs and toast to be in vain, do you?'

'No, sir. I do not.'

'I'll keep you company.'

'Gee, thanks.'

He laughed at her words and she delighted at the sound. 'You're certainly happy this morning,' she stated before taking a sip of her tea. 'Mmm. Perfect.'

'You can have coffee before clinic starts but I thought tea might be a nicer, more relaxing way to help you wake up.'

'Thank you.' She gestured to the tray. 'This is very thoughtful.' And it was. Even though she'd spent a lot of time with Felix since they'd met, there were only a few occasions where she'd witnessed the 'real' him, as though he felt the need to keep his inner being hidden from the world. Yet this morning it seemed he was happy to fling open the doors to his inner soul and let the sun shine.

She picked up the knife and fork and began eating the food before it cooled too much. No sooner had she eaten the first mouthful than Felix reached over and snagged a piece of toast from her plate. 'Hey! I thought you'd already eaten.'

'Still a bit hungry,' he mentioned before munching away. And there they sat, Harriette beneath the covers, Felix on top of the covers, eating breakfast together much in the same way they had many times before but never in a bed they'd shared. The intimate setting and the absence of Chloe made Harriette feel highly self-conscious, aware of every movement he made. Some of the dreams she'd had last night started to flood back and, as Felix had featured in them in an even more intimate way than they were presently experiencing, she felt colour suffuse her cheeks.

She quickly finished off her food, then took a large drink of her tea, wanting to be done with breakfast as quickly as possible so that Felix would leave. 'All done,' she remarked.

'You haven't had your juice yet. Chloe will be most upset if you don't drink it all, especially as she slopped quite a bit all over the bench when she was trying to pour it.'

'Oh, the darling,' Harriette murmured as she started unplaiting her hair. 'It was a good idea to include her and let her help, even if she did make a mess.'

'What's that old saying? More of a hindrance than a help?'

'Exactly.' Harriette grinned as she ran her hands through her hair, loosening it up, knowing the plait would have made the tendrils wavy during the night. 'But she enjoyed being included and that's the biggest thing at the moment.' When Felix didn't make any further comment, she glanced over at him to find him staring at her, his mouth open slightly. 'What?'

He managed to close his mouth but then slowly shook his head from side to side. Without another word, he leaned closer and removed the breakfast tray from her lap, placing it on the ground. Harriette continued to work the small knots out with her fingers but still watched Felix's movements, wondering what she'd done to make him stare at her in such a way. His look seemed to be one of confusion, one of incredulity, and she wasn't sure why.

When he nudged the open bedroom door closed with his foot, then sat on the bed, facing her more than before, her eyes widened in surprise. 'Felix? What is it?' Was he about to tell her something private, something personal, something important? She waited.

'Your hair...' Tentatively, he reached out a hand and carefully touched her loose hair. 'You are exquisite, Harriette,' he murmured as he threaded his fingers through the locks. 'Such a great colour.'

She swallowed over the sudden dryness of her throat and tried to talk but seemed unable. In fact, this time, she decided to keep completely quiet. Felix was close to her, his gaze taking in her slightly parted lips before flicking back to stare into her eyes once more.

'I need to know,' he murmured. 'Need to see if this chemistry is real and not just a figment of my imagination.' Even as he spoke, his voice deep and laced with desire, he continued to sift her hair through his fingers. 'Harriette?'

Was he waiting for an answer from her? 'Uh…' She stared into his eyes, amazed at the intensity she could see there, unable to form any other sort of reply.

'I haven't been able to stop thinking about our kiss, wanting more, needing more.' He stopped touching her hair and instead started caressing her cheek and neck with the tips of his fingers, the touch light and tender and intoxicatingly sensual. 'I've dreamt about you, I've dreamt about us kissing, about us being together and—' He broke off and gazed once more at her mouth, this time running his thumb over the soft suppleness as though he needed to touch her more intimately.

Harriette's lips parted and her tongue slipped out to wet her lips, licking the tip of his thumb.

They gasped in unison, the room filling with the tension of unrepressed desire.

'Harriette,' he murmured and began to lower his head, drawing his mouth closer and closer with each passing second. 'If you want me to stop…' His words were barely audible but the sound seemed to boom around them.

'Shh,' she whispered. 'Kiss me, Felix. Kiss me now.'

And as though he needed no further coaxing, that was exactly what he did, bringing his mouth to connect with hers, to explore, to taste, to fulfil the need both seemed to be experiencing. He kept the movements gentle, testing, teasing and tantalising both of them. The taste of her lips held a hint of saltiness mixed with sweetness mixed with perfect Harriette-ness.

She placed her hands on his arms as though ensuring he kept his hands at her face, as though ensuring he didn't pull away, because she simply wasn't ready for him to do that. He was encouraged by her touch and, slowly but surely, he increased the pressure of the kiss, opening his mouth a bit wider and kissing her as he'd wanted to for what seemed like his entire life. No other woman had made him feel the way Harriette did, accepting him for who he'd been, for who he was now and for who he would be in the future. How was it possible that she had such a capacity to care and that she would choose him of all people to care about?

Although their kiss had intensified, she wasn't letting him rush ahead, wasn't letting him speed things up and he liked that, he liked that he could kiss her intensely but slowly, savouring every second, every flavour, every sensation she was evoking within him. She was caring and giving and now she was giving to him. The action only made him want to reciprocate, to make her feel special, to make her feel as though she deserved the utmost in happiness for the rest of her life. Whether or not he was the person to give that to her, he had no idea but the question he'd originally wanted an answer to had been answered in abundance.

With a slight groan, he eased back from her, his hands still cupping her cheeks, his breathing as erratic as hers as he stared into her eyes.

'Yep. It's there all right,' he ground out.

'Uh-huh,' she confirmed as she leaned forward

and rested her forehead against his, both of them breathing heavily. 'The attraction is awake and definitely alive...'

'And increasing with each passing moment,' he finished.

Harriette sighed. 'What do we do now?'

'That's a very good question.'

CHAPTER ELEVEN

'CLINIC' WAS THE logical answer to their question even though it wasn't the one either of them wanted. The homestead seemed to be getting louder and louder as the people who had stayed overnight started to rouse and others who had been driving in for the clinic began to arrive.

All too soon, Harriette and Felix were back at work, seeing patient after patient before packing up around midday and driving out to the next property. Chloe kept up a steady stream of chatter as they drove along, Felix taking a turn behind the wheel and surprising Harriette when he reached over and took her hand in his, giving it a little kiss before he continued driving along the straight bitumen road. When she told him to slow down and take another shortcut, he didn't quibble but instead turned off and headed across country, unfortunately needing to have both hands on the wheel again.

It was as though that kiss this morning had opened up the unaired part of Felix. He was being demonstrative, jovial, interactive and, well… happy. Even Chloe noticed the difference in him, laughing as he spoke to her in a silly voice and willingly going into his arms when he went to unbuckle her seatbelt. It was as though he'd been given a new lease of life and that night, when they'd finished the clinic, Felix and Harriette sat out on the porch in rocking chairs and watched the sun set. Chloe was snuggled on Harriette's lap and eventually fell asleep as Harriette rocked steadily back and forth.

'Another busy and eventful day over,' he murmured, shifting his rocking chair closer to hers. She couldn't believe it was only that very morning since he'd kissed her…kissed her in a way she couldn't ever remember being kissed before and seemed, for all the world, as though he was looking forward to doing it again.

'Chloe seems to be enjoying the interaction with the other kids who come to the clinics,' Harriette stated and Felix nodded.

'It's good to see her laughing and smiling and joining in.'

'She deserves happiness.'

'Yes, she does, as do we all.'

'Yes,' Harriette agreed.

There was silence between them for a few minutes, the sounds of the wooden rocking chairs moving back and forth on the wooden porch.

'What do we do now?' Harriette asked softly, echoing her question of earlier that morning.

'I'd like to start by kissing you again,' he murmured and she couldn't help but smile at the suggestion.

'I'd like that too, Felix, but you know what I mean.'

'I do but it doesn't mean we need to figure everything out straight away. We've only kissed a few times and, although I do intend to repeat the action again and again, there's no need to plan a future just yet, is there?'

Harriette pondered his words for a moment. 'I guess as you usually like things all organised and hospital corners, I just thought that—'

'I'm trying to change, Harriette. I'm trying not to live my life by logic but by emotion. I don't know how I'm going to progress but I know for now I don't want to make firm plans, to organise, to sort things out. I just want to...*feel* and you... you make me feel, Harriette.'

She smiled at his words. 'You make me feel, too, Felix. Like I can't ever remember feeling before and that's a nice thing.'

'See?' He reached over and took one of her hands in his and kissed it. 'Tomorrow, we do our last clinic, then go to Darwin, then head back to Meeraji Lake when we can discuss things.'

'OK.' She lifted his hand to her lips and kissed it in reciprocation. 'For now, though, Chloe's starting to become a dead weight and we need to leave bright and early tomorrow morning.'

'Then we'd all best get to our beds.' With that, he let go of her hand, then stood and carefully picked up Chloe from Harriette's arms. The little girl went without fuss, winding her arms about his neck and resting her head on his shoulder, not waking up at all. 'Shall we?' he asked and Harriette nodded. 'You lead the way as I can't remember which rooms we were allocated.'

'Oh. OK.' She opened the screen door and held it while Felix entered the house with Chloe, then led the way down the quiet hallway of the old homestead until Harriette opened one of the bedroom doors. She quickly pulled back the bed covers so he could put Chloe down. 'I'll get her sorted into her night clothes later,' she stated.

'She hasn't brushed her teeth,' Felix pointed out and, when Harriette shrugged one shoulder, he held up his hand as though to stop her from speaking. 'I know, I know. One night won't hurt.'

'Very good,' she praised as she covered the little girl with the sheet before turning to face Felix, smiling up at him with delight. 'You're a fast learner, Dr McLaren,' she stated, unable to stop herself from edging closer to him, wishing he would take her in his arms and kiss her goodnight.

He didn't disappoint and slipped his arms about her waist, bringing their bodies into contact. He immediately lowered his head, their mouths meeting in perfect synchronicity as though they really had been designed for each other. They continued to explore but this time he let her guide them through the tumultuous, raging rapids of desire.

'You smell so good,' he murmured as she broke off and pressed soft kisses to his neck, standing on tiptoe so she could reach.

'You taste so good,' she replied before seeking his mouth once more, the intensity of their need for each other becoming heightened with each passing second. When Felix's hand shifted to slide beneath the hem of her top, Harriette instantly stilled.

'Sorry. Too fast?' he murmured against her mouth and she eased back to look at him.

'I...uh...don't want you to take this the wrong way but...having become pregnant at sixteen and bearing the consequences, I'm...er...not in the habit of becoming intimate with someone until I know where the relationship is going.' She kept her words as strong as she could because she *wanted* Felix to continue, wanted to throw caution to the wind and see where it might lead them, but she'd also promised herself decades ago never to let herself be sweet-talked or pressured into doing something she wasn't ready to do.

'You're right. Of course you're right,' he remarked and, instead of pulling away as she'd half expected, he simply slipped his hands back around her waist and dropped a kiss to the top of her nose. 'And of course we need to adhere to lessons learned in the past. I, myself, am usually extremely cautious about the…uh…women I see.'

'Women?' She raised an inquisitive eyebrow and grinned before kissing him on the lips when he started to look worried. 'I'm teasing, Felix. Of course we both have past relationships. You don't get to our age without having them, but the past is the past and although we need to learn from it, we also can't let it dictate our future.'

'So you *do* want to sleep with me?'

'Of course I do but it doesn't mean I will. For a start, we have Chloe to consider.' They both looked at the child sleeping soundly in the bed, completely oblivious to what was happening in the room. 'And I meant what I said. I need to know where things are heading before I can let myself break down that last barrier.'

He kissed her, then put her from him. 'Just as well we're not sharing a room tonight.'

'Just as well,' she agreed and couldn't help but laugh as he took her hand in his, kissed it, then bowed and closed the bedroom door behind him. 'Good night,' she called softly, not at all sure he'd heard her.

'Sleep sweet,' he returned, equally quiet, and

Harriette couldn't help but clasp her hands to her chest and giggle with happiness. No matter what might or might not happen between herself and Felix in the near future, for the moment—right for now—she was happy, and happy was good.

The next morning, they were up with the birds and watching the sun rise as they drove. Once more, Felix had been attentive towards both her and Chloe and Harriette was pleased to see the *real* Felix, the man she'd always known was buried deep inside him, starting to venture out. Part of her wanted to know why and the other part simply wanted to accept and enjoy. If she questioned him, she risked him clamming up, which she most certainly didn't want. Instead, she tried to take her own advice and not worry, not try to think fifty steps ahead as she'd conditioned herself to do.

'Have you heard from Eddie? You haven't been able to speak to him online due to having no Internet connection out here,' Felix asked as the sun started to rise in the sky, the greys of the morning changing to muted reds, blues and greens.

'I told him before we left that it might be difficult to contact me but we should be nearing Internet and cell-phone range soon so hopefully my phone will buzz with lots of delightful messages from my boy.'

'Eddie! Eddie!' Chloe clapped her hands in the back seat and hugged Captain Gumleaf close. 'I want to talk to Eddie.'

'Hopefully we'll make that happen,' Harriette told her. 'Until then, would you like to listen to some music?'

'Yes. Music! Music!'

Harriette put a CD on, singing along with Chloe to the songs, surprised when Felix joined in, his lovely baritone blending nicely. 'You have an incredible voice,' she told him when the song had finished.

His grin was a little sheepish and he shrugged one shoulder. 'My mother used to like it when I'd sing to her. She told me I had the voice of an angel and I probably did, given I hadn't properly gone through puberty.' He chuckled and Harriette closed her eyes for a moment, not only delighted at the sound of his laughter but also the brightness in his eyes as he talked of his mother. 'I don't remember singing much after she died.

I guess I never really had a reason.' He reached out and laced his fingers with hers. 'Until now.' He glanced across at her. 'You make me happy, Harriette.' He kissed her hand then let it go before gesturing to the wide open space they were currently driving through. 'Out here, in the middle of nowhere, I can start to believe that things *can* change, that life doesn't have to be a drudge.'

'And it makes *me* happy to hear you talk that way.' She leaned over and placed a kiss to his cheek, her seatbelt restraining her from doing anything further.

'Do that again,' he stated and she did, but this time when she went to kiss his cheek, he turned his head so their lips could meet.

'Oi! Focus on the road,' she told him and was rewarded with another of his delicious chuckles. Today's drive would take them closer towards Darwin but still three or four hours out of town. The clinic was a small one, for which she was grateful, and tomorrow they would go and see Felix's father. She wondered whether he'd start to withdraw from her as the time neared for him to come face-to-face with the man who had caused him pain. She still had no idea what had transpired between the two of them all those years ago but hopefully they'd be able to restore their relationship before it was too late.

By the time they arrived at the next homestead for the final clinic, it was almost midday and no sooner were they out of the car than they were swamped by a group of anxious-faced farmers who had all been talking together in a group by the barn.

'You gotta come out with us. There's been an accident. The air ambulance has been called but it's gonna take them a while to get here. Get back in the ute,' one man said as he climbed into the back, stopping when he saw Chloe sitting there, looking at him with her big eyes. 'You got a squirt in here, Doc.'

'I know I have.'

'A squirt?' Felix asked, bristling at the other man's high-handed attitude.

'A child,' Harriette offered as Chloe started to niggle. 'It's all right, darling.'

'Sorry, squirt. Didn't mean to scare ya,' the man said and waited while Harriette unclipped Chloe's seatbelt, the child instantly throwing herself into Harriette's arms. 'My kids are inside playing. You wanna go see them?' the man continued and Harriette nodded.

'Good idea. I'll take her inside, Clem, and you can tell Felix what's happened.' She looked at Felix. 'That OK with you?'

'Sure.' He winked at Chloe and blew her a kiss, delighted when she blew one back. Harriette carried Chloe and her bag into the homestead and spoke with Clem's wife, Josie. As soon as Chloe saw the other children, twin girls who were about her age, watching her favourite television show, she instantly wriggled out of Harriette's arms and went to sit down with the others.

'She'll be fine,' Josie reassured her. 'Leave her here as long as you need to.'

'She's become quite adept at playing with other children these past few days,' Harriette remarked as she kissed the top of Chloe's head before walking towards the door. 'Thanks, Josie.' When she reached the ute, it was to find Clem sitting in the front and Felix already behind the wheel, buckling his seat belt. She quickly climbed into the back and buckled up. 'What's happening?'

'Tractor accident,' Clem told her as they drove off towards the outer paddock, leaving the other men to follow in a different vehicle. 'Aaron Smithfield. He was coming over for the clinic and decided to drive across paddock in his tractor. Not the first time he's done it and it won't be the last. Cuts a lot of time off the journey.'

'Naturally.'

'Tractor got a split in the tyre and when Aaron was changing it, the jack broke and the tyre landed on him. Leg's badly broken up. Lucky for Aaron, he had his cellphone in his pocket and managed to get an emergency call through to report it. Couple of my blokes are already out there, keeping him conscious and stuff like that, but from the reports his leg looks badly busted up.'

'Any bleeding?'

'Yeah. A bit.'

'Has he lost consciousness?' Felix asked.

'Don't know.' Clem pointed out to a large tree. 'Head over there and then turn left at the tree. I've put cattle grids in so we don't need to get out and open any gates.'

'Good.' The sooner they were able to get to Aaron, the better, and when they finally arrived it was to discover that Clem's blokes, the men who worked on the land, had erected a makeshift tent over Aaron in order to provide some shade from the hot summery sun and removed the tyre.

'We've sprayed him with some insect repellent, too,' one of the men said.

'Thanks,' Harriette remarked as she and Felix carried their emergency bags towards their next patient. 'How's it going, Aaron?' she asked.

'Feeling faint, Doc,' he told her.

'Understandable.' She took Aaron's pulse as Felix hooked the stethoscope into his ears and listened to Aaron's heartbeat. She checked his eyes and asked if he'd hit his head.

'I don't think so. I may have blacked out at some point but I don't remember.'

'Are you allergic to any medicines?' Felix asked as he took out a pre-measured syringe of morphine.

'Not that I know of, Doc. Not usually the sick type, if you know what I mean, but the wife said I had to come to the clinic and get my immunisations or else I would end up being the sick type and she wasn't gonna have me die from stupidity and leave her alone to raise the kids out here.'

Harriette ran her gloved fingers carefully over Aaron's legs, then reached for the heavy-duty scissors and cut his hard-wearing denim jeans open. Felix finished administering the morphine. 'This will help you.'

'That's a nasty fracture you've got there, Aaron,' Harriette remarked as she exposed the area, shooing away the flies. She could hear Clem talking to some of the blokes, mentioning that they had to make an area for the air ambulance to land safely.

'The closer we can get the plane to Aaron, the better,' Clem was saying. Harriette stared at the fracture for a long moment, wondering if the orthopaedic surgeons would be able to fix the badly crushed tibia and fibula. Aaron's foot had also sustained a few fractures and the area was, generally, a mess.

'How's the femur?' she asked Felix as he inspected the upper part of Aaron's leg, checking the thigh for fractures.

'It looks intact but his blood pressure isn't strong so there may be internal bleeding.'

'I'll get his leg splinted,' she remarked, but first she put a neck brace around Aaron's neck. 'Need to keep your head still so we don't do any damage to your spine.'

'Yep. Pain's going now,' Aaron said and started to close his eyes.

'Aaron? I need you to stay with me,' she told him. 'Talk to me. Tell me about those kids of yours. How many do you have?'

Felix performed Aaron's observations as Harriette stabilised the leg and his report indicated that, even though the badly fractured leg was a mess, there was obviously something else wrong. Somewhere, Aaron was bleeding internally.

'How long until the air ambulance gets here?' Felix called to Clem, a clipped and urgent note in his tone.

'ETA two minutes.'

'There's a portable stretcher in the back of our ute. Can someone get it, please?' No sooner had he asked, than it was brought over.

'Leg is splinted,' Harriette reported as she once more asked Aaron questions about his family. Aaron, in typically Aussie-outback fashion, was hanging in there, showing he was made of tougher stuff and wasn't going to give in to a little thing like internal bleeding.

'Plus, if I was to die out here,' he tried to joke, 'me missus would have me guts for garters.'

'You're not going to die,' Felix told him. 'Both Harriette and I are trained surgeons and if we have to open you up here and now in order to save your life then you can bet that's exactly what we'll do.'

'Truly? Operate in a field?'

'Plane sighted! Coming in for landing!' Clem yelled, jumping up and down and waving his arms about.

'But if necessary, the plane will do,' Felix added.

'You'll make it to the hospital in time,' Harriette remarked. 'Once we get you in that plane, we can give you some top-up fluids, which will definitely help you feel better.'

'Yeah?' Aaron sounded hopeful. 'I'm not gonna die today?'

'Sorry to disappoint you.' Harriette chuckled. Soon, they had him safely transferred to the plane, both Harriette and Felix deciding to travel with Aaron.

'If we need to operate, I'll need you there,' Felix had told her when she'd said she'd stay and do the clinic.

'Don't worry about your squirt,' Clem told her. 'We'll take good care of her.'

'We'll be back as soon as possible,' Harriette told him before the door to the plane was closed and they were getting ready for take-off. Thankfully, they were able to get some plasma into Aaron, which made a big difference to his status so that when they arrived at Darwin hospital, a team of emergency specialists waiting for them, their patient was whisked away into the care of the trained orthopaedic team.

'So...' Felix asked her as they walked through the hospital. 'How do we get back to the homestead?'

'First, we go to the cafeteria and have a coffee. Then we chat to the local pilots and see if we can't work something out.' As they headed to the cafeteria Felix looked around at the walls and smiled.

'I'd almost forgotten what it was like.'

'The walls or the feel of a hospital?'

He grinned at her words. 'The feel of a hospital. I took leave when I was notified of David's death and then, when Oscar suggested I come to

Meeraji Lake, I took a twelve-month sabbatical from my hospital in Sydney.'

'And you'll go back there when you're done in Meeraji Lake?'

'That's the plan,' he stated, but there was a hint of confusion in his tone.

'You sound a little unsure.'

'Well…' He took her hand in his and laced their fingers together. 'There have been quite a few developments in my life and, honestly, who knows what might happen? The fact remains that we're only babysitting the hospital for Daisy and Oscar and when they eventually return, it'll be time to move on.'

'But to where?' she asked.

'That,' he remarked as they sipped their coffee, 'is the million-dollar question.'

'Not back to Sydney?'

Felix frowned thoughtfully, considering the question, but before he could answer they were interrupted when someone called his name.

'Felix McLaren?' A small, white-coated doctor was headed their way, the man having a moustache and a large mop of curly dark hair on his head. 'Felix? Is that really you?'

'Myron? Wow.' Felix stood up, towering over the other man, and shook hands with him.

'What on earth are you doing in a Darwin hospital? I thought you were ensconced in the hierarchy of Sydney General for ever.'

Felix shrugged nonchalantly. 'Times have a habit of changing.' When Myron looked pointedly at Harriette, Felix quickly remembered his manners. 'Allow me to introduce my colleague, Harriette Jones.'

Myron shook hands with Harriette, smiling warmly, and Harriette found she instantly liked the man. He was bright and jovial and clearly held Felix in high esteem. 'Your ears must have been burning,' he told Felix a moment later as he pulled up a chair and sat down at their table. 'As I was only talking about you this morning.'

'Really?'

'We've had a patient come in overnight who requires an intricate hernia repair and bowel resection. I was explaining to my colleagues how you basically wrote the book on that type of surgery and it was a pity you were so far away in Sydney because it would be amazing for them to watch you perform the surgery, just as it was for me all those years ago. So…' Myron grinned at him. 'How long are you in Darwin? Feel like doing surgery?'

'Uh…' Felix looked at Harriette, then down at the table. 'I'm not licensed to practise here.'

'Actually, you are,' Harriette interjected. 'As doctors at Meeraji Lake, we're automatically granted visiting medical/surgical officer status here at Darwin hospital.'

'You're at Meeraji Lake?' Myron seemed shocked but quickly recovered. 'At any rate, it's my gain so why would I bother looking a gift horse in the mouth?'

'Actually, I have a clinic to do, plus I—'

'At least come and review the patient,' Myron interrupted, clearly not wanting to hear any excuses from Felix. Felix looked at Harriette.

'Why don't you go and I'll organise our trip back to the homestead?'

'Are you sure?'

'You don't need to ask my permission,' she told him, and before he walked away she saw that bright spark in his eyes, that lightness to his step and realised that, even though he'd made the sacrifice to work at Meeraji Lake for Chloe's sake, it was a shame that he wasn't able to do what he clearly loved, which was dealing with the difficult cases and saving lives.

He might not want to head back to the big city after his stint in the outback, but she couldn't see him *not* working in a hospital environment. He seemed to have come alive ever since they'd set foot inside the hospital and, although Darwin was nowhere near as big as Sydney or Melbourne, it was still a fairly decent size as far as cities went. He'd be able to work shorter hours, perform difficult surgeries and still spend time with Chloe. Plus there were some excellent schools here in Darwin so Chloe would be well catered for with her education.

And what would she do? Would she return to Melbourne? The opposite end of the country? Would she stay? Move to Darwin? Start afresh… afresh with Felix and Chloe?

Trying not to be swamped with an air of despondence, Harriette pulled out her cellphone and called the air ambulance and Royal Flying Doctor Service to see if anyone was heading towards the homestead where they were supposed to have started clinic almost an hour ago. There weren't any flights scheduled at the moment but they promised to give her a call if things changed. Next, she called Clem's homestead to check on Chloe and to give them an updated report on Aaron's situation.

'Aaron's brother, Paul, has a chopper on his property so he's going to fly Aaron's missus to the hospital in about two hours' time,' Clem told her after she'd had a chat with Chloe, who seemed quite happy. 'So if you and Felix want a lift back to pick up the squirt, then Paul can bring you back then.'

'Sounds perfect,' Harriette agreed. 'Sorry about the clinic. Looks like we may have to postpone it.'

'Already taken care of. People will either need to make a date in Darwin for treatment or wait until next month for the next clinic. It's no sweat, Doc.'

'Thanks, Clem. See you later on, then.' After she disconnected the call, Harriette tried calling Eddie but only got his voicemail so left him a message saying she missed him. She could really do with listening to some of Eddie's adventure

stories right now. Anything to take her mind off
how Felix was starting to tie her in knots.

She put her thoughts on hold and went in to the
ICU, which was where she presumed the sick patient would be located. Sure enough, there she
found Felix, a gaggle of nurses, registrars and interns gathered around him as he pointed to a set
of patient X-rays on the large viewing box. He
was explaining the intricacies of the procedure
and some of the interns were furiously writing
down notes. Myron was beaming from ear to ear,
as though he'd done the impossible and snagged
the biggest fish around and was proudly showing
him off for his friends. Felix was…famous. Or,
at least, in medical circles he was. She thought
back to his first day in Meeraji Lake and wondered if Patrick realised just how brilliant the surgeon who had removed his appendix really was.

When Felix glanced over and saw her standing
off to the side, he raised his eyebrows in greeting before returning his attention to a registrar
who was asking him a question. Harriette waited
patiently, listening to everything he was saying,
and when he was done, and had been thanked

for his time, he walked over to Harriette, a large grin on his face.

'I'd forgotten how much fun teaching could be. I always enjoyed educating the students… and registrars,' he said pointedly and winked at her. 'I could help you study when we get back to ensure you pass those end-of-year exams with flying colours.'

'Uh…yeah. Thanks.' It was a generous offer and she knew she should be more grateful but what she really wanted from Felix wasn't a study buddy. What she wanted from Felix was the man deep down inside him, the man who had opened up to her, the man who, she realised in that split second, had stolen her heart. She wasn't the type of woman to give her heart easily, but the fact that Felix had most certainly made an impression, and one that had caused her entire being to swell with love for him, was a miracle in itself. Stunned by the realisation, Harriette continued to stare at him, completely dumbfounded. It wasn't until he waved his fingers in front of her face and called her name that she snapped out of it.

'Sorry.'

'You were miles away.' He indicated that they

should leave the ICU so the staff could continue their work.

'Look at you,' she said as they headed back into the main corridor. 'You're loving it, aren't you?'

'I have to confess I am. I mean, I love the work in Meeraji Lake, it's a different pace and I've loved the travelling and the hectic clinics, but I do love a hospital atmosphere. It feels like home.'

'And speaking of home, or rather getting back to the homestead where Chloe is, we can get a lift with Aaron's brother in a few hours' time.' She explained the situation and Felix seemed fine with it.

'So we have a few hours to waste away in Darwin, eh?'

'We do.' She bit her lip for a moment as a thought entered her mind, unsure whether or not he'd go for it. 'Would you…uh…like to go see your father?' The frown that pierced his forehead was instant and she quickly continued. 'It means that after we pick up Chloe, we don't have to come back here and can instead head back to Meeraji Lake.'

He thought on this for a moment, his eyes darkening, and she felt guilty for quashing his happiness. Although, she rationalised, he'd known all along they were going to be seeing his father. 'Why not get it over and done with?' They were walking through the corridors and Harriette wasn't sure he even knew where he was going. What she did know was that his stride had increased, had become more determined, frustrated, much the same way he'd walked around Meeraji Lake when he'd first arrived.

'You need to see him, Felix. You agreed.'

'Do I, though? I've been doing fine for decades without any input from him.'

'He's dying. That at least deserves our compassion. He's at the end of his life with regrets and, besides, apart from Chloe—'

'He's all I have left in the way of family,' he finished as they came to the front doors of the hospital. Sighing heavily with exasperation as though he knew she was right, he walked directly to the kerb and hailed a taxi. One instantly pulled up into the designated taxi rank and he opened the rear door for Harriette. 'Shall we get this over and done with?'

Not about to look a gift horse in the mouth, Harriette slid into the taxi and was pleased when

Felix got into the back beside her. As they buckled their seatbelts, he gave the taxi driver the name of the nursing home. They remained silent in the back of the cab and although Harriette wanted nothing more than to take Felix's hand in hers, to give it a little squeeze, to reassure him, he kept his arms crossed tightly over his chest.

They arrived all too soon and, where he'd been quick to get in the taxi, he took his time getting out, paying the driver and thanking him for his time. Harriette waited on the footpath outside, feeling even more antsy when she saw the darkness in his face, the mask of protection, the closed expression. Here was a man she most certainly never wanted to meet in an abandoned alley and, swallowing over the lump in her throat, she held the door open for him.

It was something he needed to do, she knew that, he knew that but…perhaps it wasn't. As they spoke to the nurses at the desk Harriette wondered whether she hadn't made a mistake in urging him to see his father.

Grim faced, they were taken through to a private room where Mr McLaren senior was lying in a bed, an oxygen tube near his nostrils and hooked around ears that seemed too big for his leathery face. Harriette had seen death many times and she could easily recognise that Felix's father didn't have long for this world. At that moment, she *was* glad they'd come.

'It's good you've come. He took a turn for the worse this morning and we were just debating whether to call you, to see if you could come today instead of tomorrow, when you walked in the door. It's fate,' the nurse said as she brushed a soft hand over Mr McLaren's forehead.

'He's not in any pain?' Felix's words were brisk, professional, detached.

'No. We've made him comfortable.'

He nodded, then thanked the nurse, asking for some time alone with his father.

'Do you want me to go, too?' Harriette asked softly when the nurse had left. Felix's answer was to shake his head. He picked up his father's hand, as he would any patient, and checked the pulse.

'Dad?' Felix's deep voice seemed to reverberate around the quiet room but there was no response. 'Dad?' he tried again, a little louder this time, and gave his father's hand a little squeeze.

'What do you want?' the old man grumbled

and opened his eyes, staring unseeingly at Felix before finally focusing. 'Oh. It's you. Come to watch me die, eh?'

'Do you know who I am?' Felix asked, knowing full well that dementia patients sometimes became confused and, in his father's case, along with the shell shock, it was inevitable. Still, there was the chance that this was a brief moment of clarity and Felix wanted to be sure.

'Of course I do. You're Felix.' The words were hoarse but gruff and the old man glanced around the room. 'Where's David? Has he come to switch off the machines, to watch me die?' His father jerked his hand out of Felix's grasp, the brisk action causing him to cough.

'Easy, there.'

'Don't tell me what to do,' Mr McLaren managed to say between coughs.

'David's not here.'

'Then who's that? Your wife? I remember you getting married. Didn't realise she was so good-looking.' He raised his bushy eyebrows in a wolfish gesture. 'Come here, toots, and grant an old man one last kiss.'

Harriette smiled and stepped forward, obliging by kissing Mr McLaren on the cheek.

'At least you did something right, ya good-for-nothing son. Where's David? Has he come to switch off the machines, to watch me die?'

Felix glanced at Harriette briefly, both of them knowing that momentary lapses in memory were more than common at this stage. 'No, Dad. Didn't the nurses tell you? David and his wife, Sue, passed away.'

'David, eh? Gone?' He coughed. 'Soon you'll be the only one left. All alone. Just like you always wanted. You always thought you were better than us, with your fancy medical school. You ran away after driving your mother insane.'

'Dad…I didn't.' Felix clenched his jaw and tried not to look at Harriette, pain and mortification flooding through him. It was out now. The main reason why his father hated him. The old man was positive Felix had caused his mother's death, but as Felix looked at his father he knew that the one who had driven his mother to the point where she'd taken her own life was the man before him.

Felix shook his head. 'This was a mistake. I shouldn't have come.'

'No.' His father's voice sounded, a little clearer than before but still just above a hoarse whisper. 'You're useless. Just like *her*. You look like her, you'll wreck your marriage, you'll push people away when they try to help and God help any kids you have because you'll make a crappy father just like she made a crappy mother.'

'I'm done.' Felix shook his head then shoved his hands into his pockets and walked around the bed, heading for the door.

'Felix, wait.' Harriette tried to reach out to him but he avoided her touch and stormed past. She stood there for a moment or two, listening to the old man's raspy breathing. She jumped when the door opened and Felix stalked back into the room.

'Don't you ever talk about my mother that way again. She was a decent, hard-working and caring woman. *You* were the one who berated her to the point where she'd felt she had no option but to end her own life, leaving us alone, leaving us... leaving us...' He stopped, unable to continue.

Mr McLaren rasped in another breath, then

out again, coughing a few times before the next breath.

'You were a rotten father and I would rather be like her, with all her weaknesses, than anything like you.'

'That's where you're wrong, boy. You're like both of us.'

'No.' Felix's tone was vehement. 'I am *nothing* like you.' He shook his head. 'You're… You're… You're not worth it. You are *not* worth it.' Then, without looking at Harriette, he stormed from the room again. Mr McLaren took in another raspy breath, coughed twice…then didn't breathe out.

'Mr McLaren?' She pressed her fingers to the carotid pulse, but didn't feel anything. She gave him a little shake and called loudly, 'Mr McLaren? Can you hear me?' No response. No pulse. She pressed the button for the nurse and then checked the old man's pupils. Fixed and dilated.

A moment later, a nurse came into the room.

'He's passed,' Harriette announced. 'Forty-five seconds since his last breath.'

'Are you a doctor?'

'I am, but best get your own doctors to call time

of death. If you'll excuse me.' Harriette headed out of the room and looked around for Felix. He was nowhere to be seen. She headed out of the closest door and found herself walking towards a lovely little garden, where people could come and walk with the residents or spend time together as a family.

'Felix?' she called but received no response. She walked further into the garden, following the path. 'Felix?' she called again, but when she rounded the next corner she found him sitting on a bench, elbows on his knees, head in his hands. She sat down beside him but didn't say anything. She just waited.

'Has he passed?' he asked about five minutes later.

'Yes.'

He lifted his head but didn't look at her. 'I'm sorry.'

'No. You had every right to say to him what you—'

'Not that. I'm sorry I let you talk me into this. It was a mistake.' With that he stood and walked away.

CHAPTER TWELVE

'HI, MUM.' THERE was a slight delay as Eddie's voice came down the line. 'I'm back in Paris, safe and sound.'

She sighed with relief. 'Good to hear.'

There was a pause on the other end of the line, then, 'What's wrong?' There was no hiding anything from Eddie. He knew her far too well.

'Oh, Eddie,' she gasped, then blurted out the whole story of how they'd had an emergency, then they'd gone to see Felix's father and that Felix had blamed her for everything. 'And then… then…' She stopped and blew her nose. 'Then when I arrived back at Darwin hospital, it was to find that Felix had agreed to perform the surgery for the patient he'd consulted on and that he'd be doing it with loads of people watching so they could observe his technique, and that's fine but it's the way he spoke to me. It was as though I was a stranger, as though we hadn't

spent any time together, as though…as though…'
She stopped and sniffed.

'Where is he now?'

'He's still in Darwin.'

'Where are you?'

'Chloe and I are back in Meeraji Lake. We managed to get a ride back in a helicopter two days ago.'

'That would have been exciting for Chloe but… Felix left her?'

'He calls her on the phone every day, talks to her. She thinks it's great. Just like you and I and, besides, he did tell her he'll be back in a few days. He's going to stay and monitor the patient in case of complications.'

'That's logical.'

'I know. I know it is but, oh, Eddie. I've blown it. I've wrecked everything by pushing Felix to see his father. Honestly, Mr McLaren was horrible to Felix. He knew exactly who he was and he said some awful things. And then…and then… Felix blamed me, then walked away. He left me there. Left me at the nursing home. Dismissed me. Looked at me as though he didn't know me at all.'

'Mum. Mum.' Eddie tried to get a word in and finally succeeded. 'I know things seem dire now but Felix will come around. He's hurt and he has a right to be. He doesn't have the right to take it out on my mother, though, and I'll be making sure he apologises to you for that.'

'It's OK, darling.' She sniffed then smiled, pleased her boy was protective of her. 'But, Eddie, what if he doesn't come around? I love him. I love the stupid, idiotic man and there's nothing I can do about it and I have to work with him for the rest of the year and then there's Chloe and—'

'Mum!' Eddie's words cut her off and even with the delay due to the fact they were on opposite sides of the world, it still managed to silence Harriette. 'Chillax. Take it a day at a time. Go and spend some time with Chloe. Focus on Chloe. Oh, and isn't it Tori and Scotty's wedding soon?'

'Yes.'

'Go and be girls together. Do your nails. Play with hairstyles. You've never had a little girl to play dress ups with.'

Harriette sniffed again then smiled. 'True.'

'Go and be a mum to Chloe. You already love

her as though she was your own. She needs you now and if Felix needs to take a few days or a week to sort his head out, then give him the space he needs. The poor bloke's already had quite a few hectic and confronting months.'

'True.' She sighed, feeling calmer than before. 'Thank you, Eddie. Sleep sweet, darling.' Harriette ended the call then blew her nose once more before going to the bathroom to splash water on her face. She could be there for Chloe…and Felix. Even if he ended up breaking her heart in the process, surely it was worth the pain? Wasn't it?

Three days later, Harriette still hadn't heard from Felix and she was doing her best to hide it from everyone—except Eddie, but at least she could face him in the privacy of her own room. Felix had called her phone and immediately asked to speak with Chloe so he could say goodnight to her, and apparently, according to Erica, he'd called the day care a few times to speak with Chloe during the day.

'At least he's keeping in contact with her,' Erica had said yesterday when Harriette had gone to pick the little girl up from day care. 'After losing her parents, he wants to make sure she knows he's only away from her because he has to do important doctor work in Darwin.' Erica had sighed. 'That poor man, the one Felix stayed behind to operate on,' she clarified. 'He's had several complications but last time I spoke to Felix, he felt the man was finally stabilising, so that's good.'

In fact, it seemed Felix was keeping in contact with everyone in the town except for her. Tori had mentioned that he'd called to check on a few patients and to say he was getting a lift to Clem's property and would pick up the ute Harriette had left there. 'He's going to drive it back to Meeraji Lake and said he'd try his hardest to get here in time for the wedding,' Tori informed her.

Even in the pub where she and Chloe had eaten dinner the other night she hadn't been safe from talk of Felix. Patrick had been showing off his appendectomy scar.

'Just look at that neat scar. Perfect stitching, from Doc McLaren. Did you know he's a famous surgeon, published in journals and sought after by doctors all over the world? And he operated on *me. Me!*'

By the time the day of the wedding arrived,

the whole town was buzzing. Tori and Scotty were getting married in a large marquee next to the community centre. Chloe woke up in a bad mood and had a tantrum when it was time to put on her pretty dress.

'I don't want to wear a dress to the wedding and Uncle Felix said he would be here to get dressed up with me and he's *not*.' The child stamped her foot and crossed her arms huffily, pursing her lips together in a pout. 'I want Uncle Felix. I don't want you, Harriette.'

'Not you, too, Chloe.' Harriette sighed and left the child alone to calm down while she finished getting ready. She'd chosen to wear a lovely floral dress with ribbons for shoulder straps, a fitted bodice and a flared skirt. Eddie had brought it over from Paris on his last trip, knowing that Tori and Scotty would soon be getting married.

So now, as she dressed in her pretty outfit and slipped on her shoes, which had a small heel so she wouldn't sink into the grass, she reminded herself to take a photo and send it to Eddie. She'd just finished piling her hair on top of her head and was about to start putting her make-up on when Chloe came into her room, still with her arms crossed, still huffing and still not in her pretty dress.

'I want Uncle Felix!' she demanded.

'Would you like to put some make-up on for the wedding?' Harriette asked, trying to distract the child by holding out a lip gloss. 'I have a purplish one in here which will look lovely on you.'

'I don't *want make-up*!' Again the little foot stamped in protest. 'I. Want. Uncle. *Felix.*' She yelled his name throughout the house and Harriette didn't blame her. She wanted Felix here too and, although she'd already tried to explain to Chloe just why Uncle Felix wasn't here, she didn't have the energy to go through it all again.

'Me, too.' Harriette put the lip gloss down and sat on her bed. What was the use of looking this pretty if Felix wasn't here to admire her? To compliment her? To share the event with her? For the past few nights, ever since he'd been so dismissive, she'd ended up crying herself to sleep, her heart breaking in the worst way possible. It was far more painful than the broken heart she'd had at sixteen when Eddie's father had dismissed her. It was worse than when Mark had abandoned her for his career.

Seeing Harriette so despondent seemed to somehow snap Chloe out of her tantrum and she quickly climbed onto the bed beside Harriette.

'I like Uncle Felix. He's funny,' Chloe stated.

'Yes, he is.'

'He's really good to me and he gives me tea sets.'

Harriette smiled and kissed the little girl's head. 'Yes, he does.' In the end, it didn't matter if Chloe attended the wedding in her grubby shorts and T-shirt with her purple shoes on her feet and purple hat on her head. It didn't matter. Nothing mattered because Felix wasn't here to share it with them.

'I miss him.' Harriette sighed.

'Me, too,' Chloe agreed, mimicking Harriette's previous tone exactly. They both sat there for a while, content just to be. When the screen door to the house opened, neither of them moved, Harriette expecting whoever it was to call out a greeting, but nothing happened. Perhaps it was the wind that had banged the door...but there was no wind today.

Frowning, she stood and headed out into the lounge room and stopped still when she saw Felix standing there, his back to her as he peered into his part of the house, clearly looking for Chloe.

'She's in my room.' Harriette's tone was firm and impersonal even though her heart was pounding with delight. He was here. He'd come back for Chloe and that really was all that mattered. His relationship with the little girl was paramount and although she'd convinced herself that that was all she cared about, she knew as soon as he looked at her that she'd been lying to herself.

'Harriette—' He stared at her for a moment, as though drinking her in, as though needing to have his fill. The look in his eyes, one of desire and need, sparked a small light of hope within her.

'Uncle Felix!' Chloe had clearly heard his voice and came hurtling through the house, her arms open wide. Felix quickly bent down, his own arms open wide, before he scooped her up and held her close, breathing in the little girl's scent and kissing her cheek. 'I missed you, Uncle Felix,' she told him.

'I missed you, too, gorgeous girl,' he remarked, then, when she pulled back, she reached out a hand and touched the three-day-old growth of whiskers covering his face.

'You look different.'

'Sorry, princess. I haven't had time to shave.' He shifted Chloe in his arms and looked across at Harriette. 'I drove straight through after picking up the ute from Clem's. I wanted to be here.'

'For the wedding?'

'Not particularly, but don't tell Tori that. No. I just wanted to be here…with you two.'

That spark of hope grew bigger but Harriette still stood her ground. 'You can't treat people that way,' she told him, knowing he knew full well what she was talking about.

'I know. I'm sorry.' He held her gaze for a long and intense moment but Harriette needed more. As though he could read her mind, he turned to Chloe. 'Why aren't you wearing your pretty dress?'

'You promised that you would get dressed up and we could go together, remember?'

'Well, I'm going to talk to Harriette and then go and get ready so we can go to this wedding together.'

'Like we planned?'

'Like we planned,' he confirmed. With that, he put the little girl down and she ran to her room to get changed. 'Just as well the dress is one she can pull on over her head and doesn't need help from us,' he stated as he quickly crossed the distance between himself and Harriette. She'd thought, with the way he'd walked, that he was going to scoop her up into his arms and kiss her full on the mouth but he didn't. Instead, he kept his hands by his sides and lowered his head for a moment before meeting her gaze.

'Harriette, I'm sorry. I was wrong to treat you the way I did because, stupidly, I let that cranky old man who called himself my father get to me. Just as he always used to.' He paused. 'As you may have gathered, my mother took her own life, unable to live with him…or indeed the rest of us.'

'Oh, Felix.' Her heart broke for him. 'That would have been devastating for you.'

'I was already at medical school but David went off the rails. Naturally, Dad couldn't take responsibility for anything and so blamed the two of us. Then I had David blaming me because I'd left home. He kept saying that if I'd been there, Mum would have been able to cope.'

'Is that why you didn't speak for so long?'

'Yes, but thankfully, as we grew older, we realised it wasn't our fault. Poor Mum. She simply
couldn't see any other way out of the mess which
had become her life. For so long, I thought if I let
people get close to me, too close, that I would end
up being pushed over the edge like her or losing
my mind like him.'

'And now?'

'Now I realise I'm my own man. My circumstances are different from theirs and I don't have
to run from the past any more. Seeing the old
man helped me realise that. I can write my own
future.'

'Oh, Felix.'

'You keep saying that,' he remarked, looking
at her. He held his hand out to her and she immediately took it, Felix sighing with relief that
she hadn't rejected him.

'That's because your pain is my pain. Can't you
see that? When you hurt, *I* hurt, which is why I'm
so sorry I forced you to see your father.'

'It wasn't your fault, Harriette.'

'But you said—'

'I know what I said and I'm ashamed of my

behaviour, the way I spoke to you, the way I left you. Harriette…' He linked their fingers together and drew her closer, looking down into her up-turned face. 'Can you ever forgive me?'

She reached out and touched his cheek, de-lighted when he leaned closer, coveting her touch. 'Of course I can. I already have.' And she had. 'You see, Felix…' She took a deep breath, sur-prised at the nervousness she felt. She knew it was the right time for a declaration of her feel-ings, she needed to tell him, but how would he respond? 'I…um…'

'Love me?' he prompted when she had diffi-culty continuing.

Harriette met his gaze and saw the question there, as though he was desperate for her to con-firm it. 'Uh…yes. How did you know?'

'I didn't. I could only hope because I love you back. I love you so very much, my sweet Har-riette.'

Now he drew her close and pressed his mouth to hers as though saying the words wasn't enough, he needed to show her as well. 'No woman—no *person*,' he clarified, 'has ever made me feel the way you do.'

'And what way is that?' she fished.

He grinned and kissed her once more. 'You make me feel as though I'm capable of so much more. You make me see myself in a different light. You make me want to be a better man, a better parent to Chloe, a better…partner for you.'

'Oh.'

'Don't be alarmed. We don't have to rush, don't have to decide on anything right now, but I've had a lot of time to think over the past few days. I'm not sure I have it all figured out but that doesn't matter because we need to figure it out together. We can live near Darwin or another small town where there's a decent-sized hospital for me to work in. I don't need accolades for my work but I do need you and Chloe. We need to discuss our future, the three of us. Chloe needs to add her own opinion.'

'Because children have opinions. Maybe not fully formed but they have opinions neverthe-less.' Harriette kissed him.

He returned the kiss, then looked at her again. 'Does this mean you're happy to become Chloe's mother?'

'Happy? Being a mother was the best thing that

had ever happened to me and now that Eddie's off overseas, living his own life, I tried, I tried so hard not to be lonely, to focus on my career, on moving on with my life, but I was failing miserably…until you and Chloe burst into my life and filled it with sunshine once again. So of course I want to be a mother to Chloe. I already love her as though she were my own because she is just so loveable.'

'Are you sure?' His tone was earnest. 'Because…because you said you didn't want to have any more children.'

Harriette chuckled. 'No. I meant I didn't want to give birth to any more children, but if you're happy with just Chloe or you may want to adopt in the future, I'm fine with that.'

'Really?' He eased back a little and looked deeply into her eyes as though he needed to see the truth of her words reflected there. Then, as though he finally realised she wasn't dressed in her usual scrubs and that her hair wasn't falling about all over the place, his gaze drank her in. 'Wow. Dr Jones. Wherever did you get such a dress? You look absolutely stunning.'

'Paris, *mon cheri.*'

'Eddie. I should have known.' Felix kissed her neck, enjoying the way her hair was piled on top of her head, providing plenty of easy access for him.

'By the way, he's mad at you for upsetting his mother.'

'I figured as much.' He drew back and looked into her eyes. 'I'll speak to him later.'

'But he also told me that you didn't mean to hurt me and that you'd come to your senses eventually.'

'Hmm. That boy of yours is smart.'

'Yes, he is.'

'Just like his mother,' Felix whispered and kissed her once more. 'So what do you say, Harriette? Let's forget the past of our upbringings and forge ahead together with our future.'

'So long as you promise never to dismiss me again, because that's what hurt the most, Felix. I've been dismissed by everyone I've ever loved, except Eddie, and I didn't care for it.'

Felix shook his head in shame. 'I will spend copious amounts of time making it up to you.'

'Good. I'm looking forward to it.' With that, she wound her arms around his neck and kissed him soundly, glad she hadn't put her make-up on yet.

'You're not changed!' Chloe's voice stopped them in mid embrace and they both froze, wondering how the child would react to the two of them kissing in front of her. Felix was the first to speak, reluctantly slipping his arms from Harriette but reaching for her hand, as though he needed to be touching her.

'I'm sorry, princess. I'll get changed in just a moment but first, can you come here? Because Harriette and I want to ask you something very important.'

Chloe frowned at him but gave in and walked towards him, still a bit huffy. She was wearing her pretty dress but she'd put it on backwards and Harriette couldn't help but smile at the child as Felix bent to scoop her up. Then he placed his free arm around Harriette, drawing the three of them together.

'Chloe, I know your mummy and your daddy have gone to heaven but what do you think about having a new mummy and daddy?'

'A new one? You can do that?'

'Yes. Yes, you can.' He kissed her cheek, delighted at her response.

'Then I want you to be the daddy and Harriette to be the mummy. *Now* can you get changed?'

'So simple,' Harriette whispered as Felix dipped his head and kissed her.

'Yes, it is. Harriette Jones—' He stopped and let Chloe down as she was wriggling so much he was afraid he might drop her. 'Harriette Jones,' he began again. 'Will you do me the honour of becoming my wife and Chloe's mother?'

'I will. And will you, Felix McLaren, do me the honour of becoming my husband and Eddie's father?'

He grinned at that and nodded. 'I'd be delighted because that boy could surely use some discipline.' Both of them laughed, but stopped when Chloe huffed and whinged again. 'All right. All right, I'll get dressed.'

'Come on, Chloe. Let's go put our make-up on.' And that was what they did, Harriette even managing to get Chloe's dress on the right way before they left the house.

Chloe walked in the middle of them, holding their hands. 'Family, family,' she sang as she wiggled her way up the path towards the large marquee. 'Come on, Mummy.' She giggled at the word and smiled up at Harriette. 'And come on, Daddy.' She looked up at Felix and laughed some more, as though her words were the best in the world.

And they were.

* * * * *

*If you missed the first story in
Lucy Clarke's* OUTBACK SURGEONS
check out
ENGLISH ROSE IN THE OUTBACK

*And if you enjoyed this story,
check out these other great reads from
Lucy Clark*

*STILL MARRIED TO HER EX!
A CHILD TO BIND THEM
DR PERFECT ON HER DOORSTEP
HIS DIAMOND LIKE NO OTHER*

All available now!

MILLS & BOON®
Large Print Medical

December

The Prince and the Midwife	Robin Gianna
His Pregnant Sleeping Beauty	Lynne Marshall
One Night, Twin Consequences	Annie O'Neil
Twin Surprise for the Single Doc	Susanne Hampton
The Doctor's Forbidden Fling	Karin Baine
The Army Doc's Secret Wife	Charlotte Hawkes

January

Taming Hollywood's Ultimate Playboy	Amalie Berlin
Winning Back His Doctor Bride	Tina Beckett
White Wedding for a Southern Belle	Susan Carlisle
Wedding Date with the Army Doc	Lynne Marshall
Capturing the Single Dad's Heart	Kate Hardy
Doctor, Mummy...Wife?	Dianne Drake

February

Seduced by the Sheikh Surgeon	Carol Marinelli
Challenging the Doctor Sheikh	Amalie Berlin
The Doctor She Always Dreamed Of	Wendy S. Marcus
The Nurse's Newborn Gift	Wendy S. Marcus
Tempting Nashville's Celebrity Doc	Amy Ruttan
Dr White's Baby Wish	Sue MacKay

MILLS & BOON®
Large Print Medical

March

A Daddy for Her Daughter	Tina Beckett
Reunited with His Runaway Bride	Robin Gianna
Rescued by Dr Rafe	Annie Claydon
Saved by the Single Dad	Annie Claydon
Sizzling Nights with Dr Off-Limits	Janice Lynn
Seven Nights with Her Ex	Louisa Heaton

April

Waking Up to Dr Gorgeous	Emily Forbes
Swept Away by the Seductive Stranger	Amy Andrews
One Kiss in Tokyo...	Scarlet Wilson
The Courage to Love Her Army Doc	Karin Baine
Reawakened by the Surgeon's Touch	Jennifer Taylor
Second Chance with Lord Branscombe	Joanna Neil

May

The Nurse's Christmas Gift	Tina Beckett
The Midwife's Pregnancy Miracle	Kate Hardy
Their First Family Christmas	Alison Roberts
The Nightshift Before Christmas	Annie O'Neil
It Started at Christmas...	Janice Lynn
Unwrapped by the Duke	Amy Ruttan

1116 LP 2P P2 Medical